Prove Yourself a Hero

The hands descended on his face, suffocating him, stifling his screams with mouthfuls of woollen windings and mufflings until he could feel all the panic, literally stuffed down his throat, exploding in his breast. He was out of control and knew it, fighting with his own terror which he knew was more dangerous in the confined space than anything further that his assailants could do to him.

In this tense and thrilling novel, K. M. Peyton's narrative gives the reader an illuminating insight into the behaviour of different people under stress—the victim, those who care about him, and those who are inflicting harm on him.

Kathleen Peyton grew up in the London suburbs and always longed to live in the country and have a horse. Although she wrote stories for her own entertainment and had her first book published when she was fifteen, she always wanted to be a painter, and when she left school went to Kingston Art School and later, when her family moved, to Manchester Art School. Here she met her husband, Michael, a graphics artist and cartoonist. They have worked together all their lives, choosing to live in Essex in order to be near good sailing, and to London. They have two daughters. Kathleen Peyton is the author of the Flambards books and winner of the Carnegie Medal.

Prove Yourself a Hero

Other books by K. M. Peyton

Flambards
The Edge of the Cloud
Flambards in Summer
Flambards Divided
A Midsummer Night's Death
A Pattern of Roses

Prove Yourself
a Hero

K. M. Peyton

OXFORD
UNIVERSITY PRESS

OXFORD
UNIVERSITY PRESS

Great Clarendon Street, Oxford OX2 6DP

Oxford University Press is a department of the University of Oxford.
It furthers the University's objective of excellence in research, scholarship,
and education by publishing worldwide in

Oxford New York

Athens Auckland Bangkok Bogotá Buenos Aires Calcutta
Cape Town Chennai Dar es Salaam Delhi Florence Hong Kong Istanbul
Karachi Kuala Lumpur Madrid Melbourne Mexico City Mumbai
Nairobi Paris São Paulo Singapore Taipei Tokyo Toronto Warsaw

and associated companies in Berlin Ibadan

Oxford is a registered trade mark of Oxford University Press
in the UK and in certain other countries

British Library Cataloguing in Publication Data available

Cover illustration by Sam Hadley

ISBN 0 19 275088 7

Typeset by AFS Image Setters Ltd, Glasgow

Printed and bound in Great Britain by
Cox & Wyman Ltd

To Peggie and Cecil

1

Afterwards, when they asked him, Peter found it very difficult to remember exactly what had happened. It was all so completely ordinary. Cycling home from school, a bit damp still from swimming, he had met Jonathan Meredith, also on a bike, cycling home from his guitar lesson with Hughie down the Mount.

'How's the old plink-plonk then?' he had asked amiably.

'Not nearly as easy as you think,' Jonathan said, 'I'm going to pack it in.'

'Stick to quads,' Peter advised, meaning horses, the only thing they had much in common. Jonathan, being a Meredith, didn't go to the local comprehensive, but a smarty school which only let him out for cautious weekends. It wasn't a weekend now.

'Why are you at home?'

'Founder's anniversary. We always get it, third week in September, a Thursday and Friday.'

All right for some, Peter thought, although—to be fair—Jonathan didn't like his smart school and was campaigning to move into the Sixth form of Peter's lowly comprehensive in order, as he put it, to learn a thing or two. But his unlowly parents were not very keen on the idea. To put it mildly.

Jonathan grimaced into the wind and changed gear for the long hill out of Hanningham. His bike had eleven gears to Peter's three (and second didn't engage as often as

1

not). Peter reckoned this marked out their relative stations in life.

This was where the plumber's van passed them. The road was not much used and they rode single file while it passed and then pressed on together. Peter switched his dynamo on, for it was a dull evening and Jonathan said, 'Blast,' because his didn't work. So much for his superior bicycle. A hundred yards farther on they came to the van parked, and as they passed a man stuck his head out of the window and said, 'I say, d'you know if this is right for Ravenshall Court?'

'Yes,' Jonathan said.

'It's on this road, is it? Or a turning off?'

'Several turnings,' Jonathan said. 'It's where I'm going. I live there.'

'Well, in that case, mate, put your bike on the roof rack and you can get in and show us. Save you a bit of leg work.'

Jonathan dismounted and bent to lift up his bike. Then, holding it, he hesitated and said, 'What are you going there for?'

'Got a burst in the stable-yard. Water main. They rang up old Arthurs but he was on an emergency already so he turned it over to us.'

Arthurs was the local plumber, well known to both boys.

'Okay.' Jonathan put the bike up.

'Bit of luck for you,' Peter said, wishing the burst had been in his stable-yard.

'Yes. See you.'

The driver of the van slid his door open and said, 'In the back—plenty of room in there,' and Jonathan climbed in. There was already another man in the front seat, the plumber's mate presumably. The van moved off immediately and disappeared up the hill at a fair speed, making Peter wonder about the expensive bicycle on top. After that he gave the incident no thought at all, until the phone rang in the middle of a whodunnit on the television and his father, answering it, said Mrs Meredith wanted to speak to him.

'Hullo?' He was a bit cross at being disturbed and went on watching the box.

'Peter? I'm just ringing to see if Jonathan is with you?'

'No.'

'You've no idea where he is, have you? He's supposed to be coming out to dinner with us tonight, to the Maxwells, and he hasn't come back from his guitar lesson yet.'

Peter was surprised enough to remove his eyes from the television and take notice.

'But he must have. I was with him, and he got a lift.'

'A lift? When?'

'Coming home from his lesson, ages ago. I was coming home from school and we were cycling together up Spinny Hill, and he got a lift with the plumber.'

'The *plumber*? What plumber?'

'The one going to mend a burst in the stable-yard.'

'We haven't got a burst in the stable-yard. Peter, whatever are you talking about?'

Peter stopped and thought hard.

'Peter, are you joking?'

'No, I'm not. It's what happened. This van stopped and asked the way to your place, so Jonathan said he was going there, and they said they'd give him a lift and he could show them the way.'

'And he got in?'

'Yes. Put his bike on the roof-rack and got in.'

'It wasn't Arthurs, was it?'

'No. They said he'd passed the job on to them.'

There was a long silence. Then Mrs Meredith, sounding very subdued, said, 'I think I'd better get on to the police. You're not going out tonight, are you? I think you might be needed.'

'No.' Peter was astonished, almost speechless. He stood there with his mouth open and heard Mrs Meredith ring off. He went on staring at the wall, trying to remember what had happened. Whatever did she think had happened? He put the receiver down and looked back at the television, where someone was just being killed. The police, had she said?

'I say, Dad.' He explained what had happened. His father was plainly interested.

'The police, eh? She's not wasting any time. What does she think he's up to? It's not very late.' He glanced at his watch. 'Half past eight. She's not a worrier as a rule.'

'It sounds as if she thinks he's been—' Peter paused, the word on his tongue too melodramatic to drop into his humdrum life—'er . . . abducted—'

Mr McNair laughed. 'What, by a plumber?'

'But he wasn't a plumber, was he? According to Mrs M, no burst at all. All a myth.'

'Mm. I see what you mean. Jonathan is the son of a very rich man, and those are the kids it happens to. Meredith's in the news this week too, if I remember rightly—some big deal in the commodities market—what was it? To do with cocoa-beans or some such. It's in the business pages—in fact he's always in the business pages. His wealth is no secret. It must have given somebody some ideas, obviously. Yes, I follow her reasoning. She's probably always been afraid of kidnappers, burglars and what have you. One of the penalties for being rich.'

Peter couldn't think of anything to say. He thought of Jonathan being pleased to get the lift, and him wishing the van had been going to his place.

'And you, presumably, are the only person who knows anything about it. So you'd better pull your wits together, boy, because you're going to have to answer a lot of questions.'

Peter felt angry because his father seemed exhilarated by the incipient excitement, rather than showing any sympathy. He felt appalled, trying to think what must have happened when Jonathan realized that he wasn't going home. Serious kidnappers, as he understood it, were pretty ruthless. Jonathan could hardly be enjoying himself at this moment. He pointed this out, coldly, to his father, and his father said, 'If the boy's worth his salt, he'll give them the slip.'

Peter thought this a stupid thing to say. 'If the kidnappers are worth *their* salt, they won't let him, surely?'

'Well, he's bold enough on a horse. He's not one of your ninny boys. I reckon he'll keep them on their toes.'

Peter decided, not for the first time, that he wasn't on the same wavelength as his father. What being bold on a horse had to do with evading kidnappers he did not follow. Jonathan might be bold on a horse because he knew horses backwards and didn't have anything to fear; but, horses apart, he was quite a sensitive lad and not much given to violence. Quite clever enough to appreciate the danger he was in. And imaginative enough not to enjoy it at all.

'You didn't recognize those fellows in the van? Get the number of the van—anything like that?'

'No. The van was a Transit, grey, pretty battered. No writing on it. I didn't get the number—why should I? And I didn't recognize the bloke, although I could give a fair description of him, I suppose. There were two blokes actually, one in the passenger seat. There might have been more in the back. Probably were, if they intended to clobber him.'

He had to say all this quite soon afterwards, when the police arrived. The house seemed very small and the evening unexpectedly painful and Peter, the centre of interest, wished acutely, in the face of so much emotion, that he could retire into a hole somewhere. He resisted emotion by habit, although a psychiatrist had once told him that it did him far more harm than good. But the obvious fear of Jonathan's parents impressed him. Jonathan's parents were two of the most formidable of the parent genre that Peter had come up against—although his own father matched up pretty well when roused. They appeared to be angry with Jonathan for accepting the lift, apparently having warned both their children about the dangers, and Peter felt bound to defend Jonathan.

'He didn't just jump in. He did ask them why they were going to Ravenshall, and they said about the burst, and then they mentioned Arthurs, and it seemed perfectly plausible. Anyone would've been fooled. I mean, I never gave it a thought.'

He had known Mr and Mrs Meredith for years, but could never recall their actually visiting the house before. They looked very strange at the dining-room table, along with Inspector Marshall and his uniformed officers and a man taking notes, and another hovering with a walkie-talkie set hiccuping in his pocket. The police had turned up in impressive numbers, no doubt because of the impressiveness of the Meredith family, who had a burglar alarm fitted which gave a warning directly to the local police station. A pity Jonathan hadn't been wired to it, Peter thought. Being so rich must be very troublesome. Father Meredith was something in the city, but, for a tycoon, a reassuringly cheerful and approachable man, happy enough to bang in posts with a mallet and erect tents and portable lavatories at the horsey events his wife was forever getting involved in. Not that he was looking particularly cheerful and approachable at the moment, hunched at the table, doodling on a note-pad with a gold-plated biro.

Marshall said to Peter, 'You're our only witness, and we can count ourselves lucky to have one at all. It could very easily have happened without anyone seeing anything. Now, we've put out a description of the van—but I'd like some information on the driver. Everything you can think of, however apparently trivial.'

Peter leaned his elbows on the table, covering his face with his hands, thinking himself back.

'Large, fair, youngish. Beefy. Not a rough type though. Fairly educated sort of voice. Brisk. Gave the impression of being an active sort of person. Wearing a navy-blue anorak with a red lining. A good one—one of those big zips in it. Outdoor sort of complexion, clean. Eyes blue, I think, and hair blondish and thick, rather untidy. Heavy jaw—the sort of man who gets fat later on.'

'Thank you,' said Mr Meredith, who was that sort of man.

'Not really like a plumber,' Peter said.

'A matter of opinion,' said Marshall. 'Did you think that at the time, or only now because of what you have found out?'

'Hard to say which,' Peter admitted. 'He didn't look particularly villainous.'

'No. They seldom do. Well done. That's not bad to go on. How old would you say?'

'Not more than twenty-five, although I couldn't swear to it.'

'Hmm.' Pause, and much rapid writing. 'No accent, dialect?'

'No.'

'What about the other one?'

7

Peter did his best, although he hadn't really noticed the mate, apart from registering that he was there.

'We'd better have a full description of the boy too. It will have to be circulated. Perhaps some photographs afterwards.'

He looked towards Jonathan's parents, who began to string his statistics together: 'About five foot ten, medium build, thinnish if anything, black hair, very curly and a lot of it, pale complexion, blue eyes . . .'

Peter was thinking: A bit of a swot by nature, a thinking man, quiet, easy, funny, lacks ambition and drive, clever, not athletic nor competitive by nature but forced into alien attitudes on a horse by sporty, single-minded mother . . . poor old sod . . . kind, but given to black thoughts about aforementioned mother, a bit soft on Mary MacArthur at Pilling Farm but too shy to do anything about it, goes to the ''Black Horse'' instead to chat up Anne Banks, the barmaid with the fabulous boobs—wrote a poem about it, very clever and funny. Wonder what Ma Meredith would say if she could read it? Poor old Jonathan, getting into the limelight for such a melodramatic reason, highly foreign to his inclinations, he the thinker, the observer, the introvert, too intelligent not to realize the danger he's in . . .

'Age?'

'Sixteen,' said Mrs Meredith.

Condition, Peter thought, fed up. How much was he worth, in pure cash? A good question. Mrs Meredith was known to be a hard bargainer in the horse world; how would she feel about bargaining for her son and heir?

'Of course, until we get a message, or some other information, we don't know exactly what the position is,' said Marshall, gathering together his papers. 'I am assuming it's a kidnapping for the time being. If we're lucky it could turn out to be some kind of a hoax. I am

8

going to see Arthurs now. I suggest you, Mr Meredith, go home and wait by the telephone, or see that someone is there ready to copy out any possible message. Observe every detail possible, however insignificant, and get in touch with us immediately if you are contacted. They will probably instruct you otherwise, but you will be wise to ignore their advice.'

'If it is a kidnapping, you understand—naturally—that my son's life is of paramount importance?' Mr Meredith stood up, looking suddenly far more like a tycoon, large and authoritative and grim.

'That goes without saying, sir.'

'I will see that the telephone isn't left.'

They exchanged telephone numbers, and the curious party broke up, the police treading out into the night to their zippy white minis and the Merediths, silent and strained, to a sombre black Rover. Peter, to avoid his father, went out after them and shut the gate and went back through the stable-yard where he stopped out of habit by Sirius's box and leant on the door, ruminating. He didn't want to get hung up with his parents and their excitement; he had done enough talking; he felt the need for a little silent cogitation, an instinctive homing of the sympathies on to the J. Meredith wavelength, which he felt must be vibrating in his direction with messages if only he had the perception to receive it; or perhaps not messages, but just general panics and cries for help and, probably—knowing Jonathan—much expletary self-condemnation for not seeing the trap he had fallen into. The Merediths were zealots for taking blame nobly. Jonathan had been schooled from an early age. If he didn't do well in a Hunter Trials it was never because the bloody horse had really messed up the water-jump or a half-witted jump judge had marked a mere hesitation as a refusal—it was always because he had got the animal wrong or lost impulsion or been otherwise inadequate. Standards were horribly high in the Meredith family. One did not fail. Hard cheese for the Meredith young, Peter thought, wishing he had seen the trap himself and saved Jonathan from a fate worse than death. Or death itself, come to that. The situation really wasn't very funny.

He put his chin on his hands, resting on the half-door, scowling into the dusky interior where Sirius was too occupied with his hay-net to investigate his owner's brooding. It was a cool, grey evening, smelling of damp and the manure heap. But nice, Peter thought, nice to be safe, leaning over the half-door, sure of his supper and the ordinariness of things. Not, for him, the things that go bump in the night. Only for Jonathan. Peter sent him not exactly a prayer, but a goodwill message, willing it into the intangible ether, hanging it on a convenient star, wishing so hard that he could feel it vibrating in the soles of his feet.

2

Jonathan *knew*, even before the van got moving again, before the door had swished to behind him, while his last foot was still moving through the air from the road to the van floor . . . but there was nothing to be done about it, so well-prepared and such smooth operators were his assailants. He didn't even see them, save as an awareness of three men converging on him. Then a gloved hand covered his eyes and another his mouth and he was forced down on to the floor, only as roughly as it took to get him there, without actual violence. But he knew that to get a glimpse of them would be invaluable, and he fought and twisted to get his head free, lashing out and kicking wildly in all directions, the only violent one amongst the lot of them. They sat on him heavily, even kindly, and a third hand, also gloved, held his nostrils until, with his mouth covered as well, he realized that he was about to pass out, and felt his body cave in without his brain's permission, a curious and rather frightening phenomenon. He lay still and they let him breathe again and taped his eyelids down with sticky tape without giving him the slightest chance of seeing anything at all. They then wound what felt like a crepe bandage over them, a very long one, tightly, round and round and round, tying it very securely, so that he knew there would not be the remotest chance of rubbing it off—even quite a job to remove it if they left his hands free. Which of course they didn't. They fixed them behind his back with handcuffs. Very professional.

'And if you're a good lad we'll leave it at that, eh?' a voice said to him out of the void. 'You keep quiet and you can be quite comfortable. We don't wish you any harm, you understand.'

He didn't say anything, thinking about it. He wasn't exactly frightened, more amazed, incredulous . . . not more than two minutes ago yakking amiably with McNair and now . . . he moved experimentally and found that the handcuffs were for real. Incredible. Not very nice really. Very tedious in fact. He wriggled himself as comfortable as possible. He appeared to be lying on bundles of something that felt like tarpaulins—no, too fine. Tent material? It felt like nylon of some sort. The blindfold made him feel very strange, in a world of his own. As if his eyes, not being able to do their own thing, were working instead on sparking off images inside the gloom. Having seen nothing he yet had a strong sense of his companions and the inside of the van. The voice which had spoken to him had been unmistakably Irish, soft and young-sounding. The other men had said very little, yet he got the impression that they were well-educated, different from the Irishman. Not excitable, but calm and intelligent. Because of the smoothness of the operation.

'What's it for?' he asked.

'It's called kidnapping,' somebody said. 'You must have read about it somewhere.'

Very ironic. And definitely educated. Public school, in fact. Smell of expensive cigarettes. How very odd. Jonathan, finding the handcuffs very uncomfortable after a bit, wriggled some more and found something smooth and flabby. He sniffed. A gumboot. Not very significant. The van was travelling fast and was very noisy. He guessed that it was probably stolen, and soon they would change to another vehicle. The police would find this van abandoned, probably revealing very little. Certainly not fingerprints.

'You're going to ask my father for money?'

'That's the general idea, matey.'

Jonathan winced inside. The situation was going to bring into play parts of his father's character much better left unchallenged, unexplored. To compel his father to declare his love publicly in terms of money was a positively spine-chilling situation, too creepy to bear thinking about. His father wasn't that sort of man. Jonathan, forcing him into this unnatural behaviour, was more worried about that than about what was likely to happen to himself.

'What if he doesn't pay?' A very likely response, Jonathan thought privately, underestimating both himself and his father.

'Don't you read the newspapers?' This was a different voice, slightly drawling, amused. 'We cut little, expendable bits off you and send them through the post.'

'Oh, shut up, Paul,' said the first voice, very sharply. 'We're not the bloody Mafia. There's no need for there to be any unpleasantness.'

Jonathan rather thought there was unpleasantness already, not liking the idea of living in darkness, and handcuffed, for what seemed likely to be a long time. Paul's remark he put down as a joke, feeling that men who sounded like they sounded wouldn't stoop to carry out such crude threats. He remained silent, having enough to think about, and nobody else said anything much. Jonathan decided that there were three well-spoken men, one called Paul, and one—the first one who had spoken—who seemed to be the boss man, whom he shortly discovered was called John. The fourth man, the one with the Irish voice, seemed to be in a different category, more as if he were employed by the smart set. When the van eventually stopped and they all piled out, save himself, the Irishman was left with him, alone. Jonathan then got

13

the idea that the Irishman was going to be his bodyguard, to watch him all the time, which proved right.

'You can call me Jamie,' the Irishman said. 'If you want anything. It's not my real name.'

'I want to go home.'

'Yeah, well, that's not on at the moment.'

'Where are we going?'

'You'll see.'

'You'll take the blindfold off?'

'No, I didn't mean that.' Jamie was muddled, almost apologetic. Not very bright, Jonathan estimated. But kindly enough. His voice was soft and worried.

'Are they paying you?'

'Sure. That's right. I just do as I'm told.'

Jonathan found it difficult to gather anything much about the changing of vehicles. They changed to what he thought must be another van, only a quieter, more expensive-sounding one. The transfer seemed to take place in a large garage, by the smell, and quite a lot of gear, including the tent-like bundles, was packed into the new vehicle. They set off again, the boss-man, John, driving. He drove fast.

'We're not going to have a lot of time to spare,' he remarked. 'It's gone half past five already.'

'The start's at half six.'

'That's what I mean. By the time we get everything sorted out—and the lad here packed up.'

Jonathan could not work this out, and decided that he didn't like the prospect of being 'packed up'.

'What do you mean—packed up?' he asked.

Jamie's voice close beside him said, soothingly, 'It won't be for long, just to get you out without anybody seeing.'

To Jonathan this sounded hopeful, indicating that he might stand a chance of attracting attention if there were

14

to be other people about, but optimism was instantly crushed by the driver saying, cuttingly, 'You don't have to answer *all* his questions, Jamie, for God's sake—the less he knows the better. You can start getting him fixed up now—we'll be there in ten minutes and we don't want to mess about. Everything else is ready to chuck out.'

'Who's got the transistor?' someone asked.

'I have. We're going to time it nicely for the weather forecast. Keep it turned up loud and that'll drown out any possible protests.'

'But we're going to gag him surely—?'

'Cripes, yes! But we can't be too careful. Just like the dress rehearsal.'

It was all quite different suddenly, the real thing, the niceties dropped. Jonathan, instinctively uncooperative, out of plain funk, had no more chance to wonder what it was all about, seized by a lot of rough hands and thrust uncompromisingly into some sort of a box, and a very small box at that, so that as he knelt, and was forced down by the back of his neck till his forehead touched his knees, the sides of the box were pressed against him on all sides, and when they put the lid down it was hard against his back and chained hands.

'Just trying it for size,' somebody said, and let him come upright again. Jonathan, no longer calm, but claustrophobically panic-stricken at the thought of being contained in such a tiny space, started to scream and struggle with such force that it took the three of them all their strength to keep him where they wanted him.

'For God's sake, shut him up!'

'Pack it in, you idiot!'

'Cripes, where's that scarf?'

The hand descended on his face, suffocating him, stifling his screams with mouthfuls of woollen windings and mufflings until he could feel all the panic literally stuffed down his throat, exploding in his breast. He was out of control and knew it, fighting with his own terror which he knew was more dangerous in the confined space than anything more his assailants could do to him. They pressed him down, angrily, their cool as much disturbed as his own, swearing and arguing and clumsy, and closed the lid hard down on his back. The whole box was thickly lined with foam rubber, and Jonathan rolled up like a woodlouse, felt himself insulated, entombed, utterly divorced from the world and all reality. He was on his own, and by his own efforts he knew he would survive, or not—an entirely salutary realization, for his desperation was using up an unnecessary amount of the meagre air supply. His own breathing was the only noise he could hear, wheezing with great difficulty through his stifled air passages; his nose, upsidedown, was having a job to cope, and needed every bit of help it could get, by his being very calm and relaxed. He knew all this, even while he could feel trickles of the hot sweat of fear running down his body. It was like being two people, the strong, implacable one, knowing what he must do, trying to crush the instinctive self, wild with fright. It was a battle on its own going on in the box, quite apart from anything that might be happening outside which at that moment truly didn't concern him. He could feel the box being moved, carried, put down, moved again, kicked. He thought he could hear people talking, the transistor radio playing, someone laughing, an engine starting up, but none of it mattered to his private struggle. The foam rubber seemed to be bulging into all the few spaces his body had left and sucking the air into its thick, hot substance, denying him his right to it. He thought only of breathing; there was nothing else to distract him. It was very hard, and he didn't see how he was going to even notice if he lost consciousness, because there was so little to show for being alive, except the spreading pain of cramps which he would be only too happy to forego. There was, curiously, no sense of time at all: time was only as long as he could breathe, and time was running out. He started to feel terribly hot, burning all over, and he couldn't hear himself breathing any more, but only his pulses thumping. He tried to ration his breathing, making it very shallow, but he couldn't hear it or feel it for the throbbing in his head, and he realized that there was nothing he could do now to help himself: it was beyond his control. The thumping and the throbbing was all there was, bursting in his ears and his throat and his eyeballs. The box no longer seemed to contain him: he was unconscious of confinement, of pain, of even *being*. Only the pounding was real, swelling monstrously, burning, killing.

Afterwards he remembered he had always thought of suffocation as an innocuous death, as deaths went. Not very intelligent really. He never thought that again. The air was cool and beautiful, smelling of the sea. He realized after a bit that the gasping, whimpering noise was himself—coming to, perhaps. He couldn't see, but he could breathe, move, even his hands. How long had he been? He was lying down, and there was a strange, unfamiliar motion beneath him, and strange noises going on. He struggled feebly on to his side.

'Thank God for that,' somebody said, close to. 'I'll leave him to you now, Jamie. Try him with a drop of brandy. He'll be OK.'

'Oh, Jesus!' said Jamie softly, not blaspheming, but in thankfulness. 'I didn't reckon on that. We nearly suffocated him. Can you hear me, lad?'

Jamie's large horny hand steadied his jaw and trickled brandy into his mouth. Jonathan was grateful for it. Gradually, not saying anything, he felt his senses returning, lying there on what felt like a bed, with a blanket over him. But the bed was moving in a very peculiar way, even keeling slightly but quite unmistakably to one side. At first he thought it was him, still half-conscious, but then he understood what it was. He was on a boat, sailing. He could hear the hiss of water past the hull and the grinding of sheet-winches from the cockpit. He also heard the distant report of a gun going off, which he associated with a racing start. Extraordinary.

'What's going on?' His voice sounded very far away and quavery. He was surprised, slightly embarrassed.

'Don't you worry about it,' Jamie said. 'Just you take it easy.'

'We're on a boat?'

'That's right.'

'Why?' Cripes, he had the father and mother of a headache! He moved his hand up to his face instinctively and encountered the all-embracing blindfold, groaned angrily at his lot.

'Can't I have this off?'

'No, you can't, lad. And if you meddle with it I'll put your hands behind your back again.'

'It smells.' It did too, of something Jonathan was familiar with, but couldn't quite place. He didn't like the idea of being permanently blindfolded, but certainly didn't want to be handcuffed again. Wasn't much he could do about it. Besides, if they were on a boat, he wasn't going far on his own.

'Where are we?'

'God knows. It's some race or other, across the North Sea. They thought it would fill the time in, while your father gets round to paying up. Keeps you out of the way. Nobody's going to find you out here.'

Too true, Jonathan thought. God, he felt terrible! As if he had just completed a marathon race. He lay listening to the swish of water past the hull, a gentle, pleasant, rhythmic noise with the occasional slap of a larger wave, accompanied by the tapping of sheets and blocks and voices out in the cockpit. He lay thinking about it for some time, too surprised about what had already happened to be any more surprised at finding himself at sea. What a peculiar day it was turning out to be. He felt very tired and could easily have gone to sleep. The motion was very quiet and easy, not much wind, and presumably they were still in the river. He presumed the river Blackwater at West Mersea, or possibly Burnham-on-Crouch, or even off Harwich—hard to judge. From where they had picked him up the distances were much the same to each. But what race it could possibly be starting on a Thursday evening so late in the season he had no idea. Perhaps something experimental, or some club event. Jonathan knew quite a bit about racing, his father having several yachting friends. No doubt some of them would know what race it was. Very likely some of them were in it, sailing a few hundred yards away on the same course. Cripes, what a situation!

'Are you on the trip just to watch me?' he asked Jamie. 'Or do you have to crew as well?'

'No. I just watch you. That's my brief.'

'All the time, day and night?'

'You've got it.'

'Have you sailed before?'

'No.'

He might be sick, Jonathan thought hopefully. Totally incapacitated. So might he, come to that.

'Very boring for you.'

'I'm getting paid.'

The more he thought about it, the more clever the kidnapping appeared. Jonathan was impressed. Even the getting aboard: the case they had packed him in must have been a life-raft case, at the best so heavy that it was a

19

full-time job for two men to lift, and an essential part of the gear of a racing-yacht. Nobody would have looked at it twice, no doubt lending a helping hand to get it into the launch to go out to the yacht, helping to hoist it aboard. It would have aroused absolutely no suspicion at all, probably wouldn't even be remembered if the police went round questioning. If they *did* go around questioning. Jonathan did not see that there was anything to lead them to the boat at all. There would only be Peter's evidence, and they had been convincing plumbers.

Having done that much thinking, in the space of about one minute, Jonathan was a bit appalled at what the future held for him. Not so much danger as infinite, crashing boredom. Even an exercise in plotting escape was futile: he wasn't that good a swimmer. No prospect of helping to crew, or even reading a book. For how many days, had Jamie prophesied? Three, presumably, before the yacht returned to base. Seventy-two hours—unless an opportunity to scarper presented itself on the other side, where the harbour would be crawling with British yachts and yachtsmen. Again, unlikely, with these so well-organized kidnappers. He guessed, without much joy, that they would drug him for the period in harbour, and hide him up in the forepeak.

To think up that much had occupied about another thirty seconds. Only seventy-one hours and fifty-eight and a half minutes to go. Jonathan curled over on to his side, mentally shut his already shut eyes, and went to sleep.

3

'Well, yes, it is serious. Not a joke at all. That's what I've come to tell you.'

Mrs Meredith got out of her car in the McNair stable-yard where Peter was mucking out Sirius's box.

'We've had a letter. I rang the inspector and told him and I have to see him at ten o'clock. I thought I'd call in here on the way as I'm early. I just can't sit about, I'm afraid. Do you want to have a look at it?'

She held it out. The message was typed on a perfectly plain piece of white paper and said quite simply: 'We want £500,000 for your son's return, to be delivered according to directions you will receive tomorrow. If we do not receive it, he will be found drowned.'

Peter didn't know what to say. He had never been in the position of having to comfort someone of Mrs Meredith's calibre before, and didn't know how to begin. She looked haggard and hollow-eyed, but rather more angry than grieved. All he could think of to say, for some ridiculous reason, was, 'Hard cheese,' which didn't fit the bill at all. In fact, the threat in the letter was chilling, to put it mildly.

'I suppose the police will try and interfere, but quite honestly I would far rather hand over the money and have done. I just couldn't bear to run any risks. I'm not at all tough when it comes to this sort of thing. The waiting about is really horrible, not knowing what on earth they're doing with him.'

'My father's in the office, if you'd like to see him,' Peter said, terrified she was going to cry. 'Come and have a cup of coffee—you've got time.'

The stable-yard office was plushy, with central heating and chrome and leather armchairs for prospective customers and an electric percolator which only needed plugging in. Peter plugged it in. Mr McNair got up from his desk and asked for the news.

'Oh, Christ, that's not nice.' He read the note, rubbing his hand anxiously round his stubborn jaw. Peter watched him, wondering what he would be feeling if it was his own son that had been kidnapped. McNair was far more serious now, probably thinking the same thing. They didn't love each other very much, father and son, but a bolt from the outside world like this put a different complexion on the relationship. It made one think about things that one would ordinarily rather not. Peter didn't, taking coffee cups out of the wall cupboard.

'I'm worried about the way the police might want to interfere,' Mrs Meredith said. 'I told Peter, I would rather simply pay out, however cowardly it might seem.' She paused and added, 'This current deal of James's—the newspapers are making a lot of fuss about it, and I suppose it gave somebody an idea. Or it might be somebody who has been working it out for some time, for it seems to be very cunningly planned—knowing that Jonathan would be home this Thursday, for example, when ordinarily he would be at school.'

'It was very smooth, the way it was done,' Peter said. 'Not a bit suspicious.'

'Quite, and not a sign of any of them since, not a clue of any sort.'

'And catching Jonathan on his way back from his lesson—he always goes on Thursdays when he's home. They probably knew that. Which means they must have been watching him and working it out.' Peter was impressed. 'They're *clever*.'

'Yes, I think so,' said Mrs Meredith. 'It makes it far more tricky, I'm sure. I shall have to discuss all this with the Inspector.'

Peter wondered about the threat in the note, but didn't like to mention it. Why drowning? That might be a clue. As if sensing his thoughts, Mrs Meredith said, 'And the threat they use in the note, nicely calculated to get us moving. All worked out, manner of death specified in advance. I really don't like it.'

In spite of her brisk, sensible manner, her face seemed to tremble; her firm thin lips turned down involuntarily and she gave a sort of hiccup. Peter busied himself with the coffee, feeling desperately embarrassed, and angry with himself for it, for it was easily bad enough for even a toughie like Mrs Meredith to break down. His father, much more worldly, went round the desk and said, 'There, Elizabeth, don't upset yourself. They don't stand much chance of getting away with it, you know. I'm sure you've faced stickier hurdles in your time.'

'No, Arthur, I haven't. Use your imagination,' Mrs Meredith said, with perfect justice. (But Peter knew his father hadn't got any.) 'The last time I cried was when Major was put down, and this is far worse, believe me.'

'It'll work out all right, I'm sure. The police are bound to find something out today. God, gel, he might be back home with you tonight and you'll all be laughing about it!'

'Well, I hope you're right.'

Peter poured out the coffee, the nasty moment overcome, and handed the milk and sugar. He was still thinking about the drowning: that Jonathan was a fair enough swimmer, and he wouldn't drown in a pond or a river, only in the sea, far out. Which meant from a boat.

23

Unless, of course, they knocked him on the head first, or held him under. But the boat idea was strong in Peter's mind. It didn't want to go away. Telepathic vibrations from J. Meredith himself, Peter thought. If they were clever, they would want the death to look like an accident. But if they were clever, there would be no death. Peter thought that Inspector Marshall probably had more system than he had when it came to working out the possibilities, but he thought a boat came into it somewhere.

At that moment the telephone rang. It was the police.

'They want you to go over and look at their picture-book,' Mr McNair said to Peter. 'Photos of villains. See if you recognize the driver of the van.'

'He can come in with me,' Mrs Meredith said.

Peter kept his face from showing his disinclination at the prospect. He had been going to ride Sirius. There was something abrasive about Mrs Meredith—her company was like being put into a box of pins. He went to fetch an anorak more respectable than the one he had been mucking out in, and went out obediently to the car. No wonder Jonathan mutinied at times, he was thinking, as he said polite, non-committal things. She wouldn't have things any way but her own. She was ruthless and incredibly bossy, and it was hard to believe now that she had shed a small tear for Jonathan a few minutes ago.

'It is so *underhand*,' she was saying. 'A despicable crime. One can have no sort of sympathy at all for people who manipulate the innocent—'

She manipulated, Peter thought.

'Yes, I agree that we're up against brains,' Marshall conceded at the end of the morning after Peter had drawn a blank. 'There's very little we can do until things start to develop from their end, another communication, perhaps. This one, I'm afraid, tells us very little. Central London postmark, standard paper, envelope, typing . . . almost

24

nothing to go on, save that it is an educated message. We are treating this as absolutely top priority, Mrs Meredith, rest assured.'

Rest assured. Peter remembered the words, not resting assured at all, unable to think about anything else. His father had him schooling green horses all afternoon, but—due to lack of the required concentration—he ended the session with an abrupt and painful collision with a telegraph pole when the horse he was riding shied at a cock pheasant, slipped and fell, shooting him off over its shoulder, and kneeling on his ankle for good measure. Peter got up slowly, muttering foul oaths, and his father caught the horse and came and looked him over doubtfully.

'It's no good riding a brute like this as if it's a lady's hack,' he said. 'Your mind's not on the job.'

'No, it bloody well isn't.'

'Well, you can't leave it now. Show it who's boss—twice round the field nicely, and then we'll call it a day.'

'I can't walk,' Peter said, discovering the fact.

'I'll give you a leg up.'

Twice round the field nicely took half an hour and much patience, by which time Peter's ankle was thickening ominously inside his boot and he got worried about getting the boot off. His father effected this for him back in the stable-yard with a cheerful 'We've got to be cruel to be kind' which left Peter pale and speechless. At least he got out of doing evening stables, and went indoors to watch the news on the television, propping his foot up on the sofa. The last item of news caused him to sit up sharply. 'Following the disappearance yesterday afternoon of sixteen-year-old Jonathan Meredith, son of the city businessman James Meredith, Essex CID, who are investigating, suspect kidnapping. Jonathan was offered a lift in a grey Transit van two miles from his home,

Ravenshall Court, in Essex, and has not been seen since. It is understood that his parents have received a message demanding the sum of half a million pounds with a threat that if the money is not paid Jonathan will be drowned. In spite of intense police activity all day no clue as to the whereabouts of the missing boy has been found. Inspector Marshall, leading the investigation, says that it is being treated as one of extreme urgency.'

Peter, scowling, got up to turn the box off and found that he couldn't use his rolled-on leg at all. Further scrutiny showed that, having got his boots off, he was going to have to go to bed in his jodhpurs, or unpick the seam, at the rate his ankle was swelling up. He was annoyed and sat looking at it gloomily, until his stepmother came in and said, 'Why you sitting around, hey? The stables is done?'

'No.' He waggled his toes at her, the only part of his leg he could move, and she said, 'Oh, you poor leetle bugger. What is happened?'

His stepmother, an ample cheerful Italian lady, having picked up English as best she could, had picked up a lot of the wrong words but, not interested in moving in polite society, only in working in her kitchen, it was no embarrassment for the most part. She was homely and sympathetic and Peter had been known to weep on her ample bosom in days gone by, which is more comfort than Jonathan, he was willing to bet, had ever received from his scrawny parent. She unpicked his jodhpur seams and he sat in his underpants with his foot in a bowl of water floating twelve ice-cubes, eating spaghetti bolognese and feeding titbits to his year-old brother who went by the unlikely name of Giovanni McNair.

Jonathan, he thought, where are you now?

But there really wasn't anything to be done.

4

Jonathan, who had enjoyed what little sailing he had done, was quite prepared to make the best of a bad job, but found that the blindfold effectively turned him zombie after some hours. After a miserable period, handcuffed while Jamie slept, close to panic and with a vile headache, he eventually came to terms with his situation. 'Lots of people are blind,' he acknowledged. 'They cope.' His other senses, even after only an hour or so, sharpened to compensate. Even the smell of the damned bandage, after a long period of concentration, was traced to its source: Radiol liniment, used on horses' legs. It was a stable bandage. It fitted, for Jamie, with his soft Irish voice and soothing manner, could well have been a groom. He called John, the boss man, sir. It occurred to Jonathan then that, by using his other senses in their newly sharpened form, he might well, if he were clever enough, deduce quite a lot about his companions which could well prove useful. There was nothing else to do, after all.

But why, if his kidnapper was rich enough to employ a groom and race a yacht, was he stooping to kidnap for money? Just another sport? To relieve the boredom?

'Although you will hear us calling each other John, Paul, and Ringo, those aren't our real names, you understand,' John told Jonathan. He took the handcuffs off him. Jamie had woken up and was cooking bacon. Ringo was on the helm and John and Paul had come down for breakfast. Breakfast?

'What time is it?' Jonathan asked.

27

'Seven o'clock?'

'Friday morning?'

'That's it. We've practised for this. We've been calling each other John, Paul, and Ringo for weeks.'

Nutters, Jonathan decided. Or merely scrupulously careful.

'Do you want to wash? There's some hot water left over.' John, by the scraping noise, had been shaving. He put a slab of soap in Jonathan's hand, draped a towel round his neck and said, 'The water is in a bowl in front of you.'

Jonathan already knew that. He was a better blind man than he knew. He could smell the warm plastic of the bowl and hear the water slopping as the boat slid down the side of a wave. There was bacon sizzling, a kettle near boiling, the smell of after-shave, of wet oilskins. All very domestic. He washed his hands and the part of his face uncovered, and dried himself on the towel. John then guided his hand on to a hot mug of tea and said, 'Sugar?'

'Yes, please. One.'

It was crazy.

He sat resting his elbows on his knees, the mug in his hands, moving to the motion of the boat. She was sailing eagerly on a reach, very comfortable.

'Is this your boat?' he asked.

'No.'

'Is it stolen?'

'No.'

'Borrowed?'

'That's right.'

The tea was marvellous, raising morale a hundred per cent.

'Bacon and egg?'

'Yes, please.'

'I'll put the egg between some bread, so you can manage. The bacon's there. Okay? I've put salt on.'

The voice was smart and brisk, London stockbroker type. Youngish. If—having chosen the names John, Paul, and Ringo for pseudonyms—he was a teenager during the Beatles period, it made him in his middle twenties, give or take a few years. Jonathan found that he had quite a strong picture of him in his head, but whether it was the true one or not it was impossible to tell. He was certainly young, active, decisive, practical, and very sure of himself. He had also, Jonathan began to realize, planned the kidnap with enormous attention to detail.

Paul's voice was slightly affected, with a public-school lengthening of the syllables such as 'orf' for 'off', and he seemed more of an indolent nature than John. He was in charge of the navigation, which he seemed to find easy enough.

'The log reading is sixty-two miles. Lousy progress. But at least the wind is freshening now. We might begin to move before long.'

'Where are we going?' Jonathan asked.

'You ask too many questions,' John said, quite sharply. 'It would be far better if you shut up.'

Jonathan decided that the boss man was not as kindly disposed as he had been thinking.

'We mustn't get friendly,' Paul said, 'in case the whole jolly plan fails to work and we are obliged to—'

'Look, Paul, that's not necessary. Just shut your face and concentrate on getting there as fast as possible.'

'Obliged to what?' Jonathan said, wondering if his guess was right.

'Shut up!' John said, in a voice that no one was likely to disobey.

Jonathan supposed that it was, and gloom set in again. It didn't do to dwell on likely developments, if he wanted to keep up his front of British phlegm, which he thought he was doing quite well so far . . . apart from the bit when

29

they shut him in the life-raft case. Cripes, if they tried that again . . . the egg sandwich stuck in his throat, and he had to swig it down with tea. Even the thought of it made his body tingle with fear. He removed the idea from his mind, along with the other one, and tried to think of something to cheer himself up. He couldn't. He sat back with his tea. He wondered what they were doing at home, and wished he was in his own bed listening to the woodpigeons in the pear tree. For a moment he felt close to tears, like a four-year-old. He didn't want to be murdered: there were too many things to do first. He wanted to die calmly in bed when he was eighty, some time in the far-distant third millenium. He wondered if there was a great search out for him yet, and whether it would be in the newspapers. It would be if they killed him. At least Peter saw him go, which was a bit of luck, otherwise there would have been no clues at all. Jonathan, steeped in self-pity, lay back on his bunk again and clasped his hands behind his head. The only comfort was that he couldn't wash up. Jamie had to do it.

John and Paul went back on deck and Ringo came down for his bacon and eggs, but didn't say much. He was in any case much quieter than John and Paul; his voice was soft and gloomy, and Jonathan got the impression that he wasn't very convinced about what they were doing. But he seemed to know the most about sailing the boat, for John, although the boss, deferred to him in the matter of sail adjustments. Jonathan decided that the boat perhaps belonged to Ringo. Certainly Ringo knew its ways better. He offered Jonathan a cigarette which Jonathan accepted out of strategy rather than desire, for he thought if it came to the push, Ringo might prove the sympathetic area. Ringo lit it for him, and put it to his lips.

'Thanks.' The yacht was beginning to travel with the wind freshening. He sat up and tried to wedge his feet across on the opposite bunk, but it was too far away, which suggested that the yacht was fairly big, about forty foot at a guess.

'What time do you expect to arrive in—wherever we're going?' John was out of the way on deck, and perhaps Ringo would answer a few questions.

'Oh, this evening, I daresay. Depends on the weather.'

'Then we stay the night and start back again?'

'Probably. Got to be back Sunday.'

'Are there many boats in this race?'

'Umm—about twenty-five, thirty perhaps.'

All those British yachtsmen to rescue him, if he got the chance! It would surely be on the news broadcast by six o'clock—his father was quite a newsworthy man—and quite a lot of the yachtsmen would know him. Jonathan felt more optimistic.

'What yacht is this?' Nothing like pushing your luck.

'Are you joking? This is a mystery trip as far as you're concerned.'

Blast him. 'What class is she in?'

'Class One.'

He was right about her size. Over forty foot.

'Has she won much?'

'No.'

That was as much as he got out of Ringo, apart from the cigarette. He toyed with the idea of using the cigarette to set fire to the bunk cushions, but did not see that it would advance his cause overmuch, besides which Jamie was still on guard. He tried Jamie with a bit of chat about horses and discovered that he was certainly knowledgeable on the subject, although not to be drawn on particulars— no doubt having been well-briefed by John. He knew enough to fit in with the hunch about his being a groom, especially about racing.

'Do you know my mother's horse, Florestan?'

'Aye, I've seen it run. It's a useful animal.'

That was the only informative reply he achieved, proving that Jamie was to be found at the local point-to-points, for that was where Florestan appeared in public, nowhere else. Fed up and bored, he lay back on the lee bunk again and listened to the buffeting of the water on the hull beside his ear, his body adjusting to the swoosh down the big waves and the jerks through awkward tops, braced, dropped, thrown—a very unrestful bed. Jamie started to groan. It was cold and clammy, with the smell of old cooking and diesel fuel sloshing about in the tank and damp cushions; wet oilskins when somebody came below, a whiff of gas as the stove was lit for tea. The hours ran into each other. The men were much occupied with sailing and Jamie was sick, so Jonathan undid the blindfold and started to ease it off but Jamie, groaning still, saw him in time and swore at him and knocked his hands away. Jonathan, frustrated and foul-tempered, lashed out, bringing up his legs and kicking out wildly. Jamie's shouts brought reinforcements and wet cold hands in force; Jonathan was handcuffed again and didn't even get a cup of tea the next time round, and could do nothing but lie and listen to the screeching of the wind and the crashing of a loose bottle in the booze cupboard. But he had sailed before and knew that it always sounded awful below. He wasn't afraid for his life in that direction.

He dozed off eventually, in spite of being so uncomfortable, and awoke with splitting cramps in his confined arms some undefinable time later. He was immediately wide awake, the pain very sharp, but after one instinctive convulsive thresh about for freedom—in vain—he realized that a conversation was going on round him.

He instantly dropped quiet and made his body flop out again, breathing heavily, and his acting was rewarded by

32

an accolade from John himself: 'Thank God he has the sense to pass the time sleeping instead of being sick all over the place like you, Jamie. I thought you said you were never seasick?'

'Not on them Channel ferries, so help me. I thought it was the same thing.'

Cheerful, unsympathetic laughter, and a condescending, 'Well, it's always worse below. But I'm afraid you're lumbered. That's what we're paying you for.'

'Sure. I'm not complaining. As long as that's all I've got to do. Nothing unpleasant like.'

'No. With luck it'll work out. Not that I'm changing my plan if it doesn't. Don't get that idea. They will just have the one chance to pay out, no more. This is a weekend job, short and sharp, and if it's no deal on their side tomorrow night, he goes in the drink and we go ashore in the clear.'

Paul's drawling voice, still amused, said, 'Waiting for the message to come through will be the nastiest part. Two in the morning, the lowest ebb of the human soul.'

'My soul's at pretty low ebb now. How about a snifter? We don't actually care whether we win this race or not, do we?'

'Ask Ringo. I doubt it. He's not used to winning.'

'I reckon we'll win where it matters. We'll drink to it. Water in yours?'

'No. Thanks.'

'Whisky, Jamie?'

'Not this time.'

'Yes, please,' Jonathan wanted to say, chilled by what he had heard. He had got the message before, about his being murdered if the money wasn't forthcoming, but this time it had been spelled out, time and place, and he couldn't pretend that it was a figment of his imagination. These weren't bungling peasant black-

33

mailers, but sophisticated, highly-organized and clever young men. He did not now doubt for one moment that what John had just said would happen, if his parents didn't pay. They would have failed in their mission; he would have disappeared, but as far as he could work out there would be absolutely no shadow of suspicion to fall on them. Admiration of their superior plotting did nothing to lessen his fear. If the success of the venture or not was to be communicated in the wee small hours, as Paul forecast, nobody would be more interested in the result than himself, and nobody's soul would be more sick. It was sick now. The thought of being dropped in the North Sea forty or so miles from land was not pretty. Jonathan found it difficult to feign sleep under the circumstances. He turned his head into the cushion to hide the sudden tremor of the no longer stiff upper lip, and the cramps in his arms made him groan out loud.

'You awake, lad?'

They took the handcuffs off again and sat him up and gave him strong tea laced with whisky. For prospective murderers they were kind and cool and cheerful, and Jonathan was glad he didn't have to work hard at disguising his expression. With so little of it showing, he could afford to forego the effort. He drank gratefully, his teeth chattering slightly against the mug. He was very cold and felt rather sick. The thought of quite possibly only having another thirty-six hours or so to live was not conducive to a feeling of well-being.

John said, 'We should be in harbour in another hour or so. That thought cheer you?'

'It would if I thought I was going to see anything of it.'

'Your luck's out, mate. But it'll be nice and peaceful for you.'

By coercion, no doubt. 'I've been asleep all day. Most of it anyway.'

'Best way to travel. You should be grateful. For a kidnappee, you know, you're getting very high-class treatment.'

So far.

'What happens when we get into harbour?'

'Well, we're going ashore for a meal. You will stay here with Jamie.'

Jonathan decided that there were distinct possibilities in that arrangement and felt slightly more optimistic. Wherever it was—Ostend? Breskens?—it would be swarming with allies if only he could get a message across. If he were clever enough he might be able to outwit Jamie. Jamie was not very bright, and was now weakened by a long period of seasickness.

Ringo's voice called down from the cockpit: 'How about a spot of all hands on deck? It's bloody busy out here, and I reckon we can put the big jenny up again. Wind's dropping.'

'How long before we're in, do you reckon?' John asked Paul, getting to his feet to answer the summons.

'Under the hour with luck, unless the wind dies.'

'You know the drill then, Jamie? Half an hour before we're due in—'

'Aye. You let me know when you think fit. I'll see to it.'

'Okay. '

'Cripes, them steamers—! We'll not get run down?'

'Don't worry, Jamie. It's simpler than horses.'

'God Almighty, give me horses any day.'

The heavy thumping of turbine engines was louder now than the hissing and crashing of water along the hull. The sea was easier, suggesting that they were getting into sheltered water, and the mournful tolling of a bell buoy bore out the theory that they were going into the mouth of a commercial river. Jonathan guessed the Schelde, which meant Breskens.

'What's the time?' he asked Jamie.

'Nearly seven.'

Friday evening, a twenty-four hour crossing. It fitted. Jonathan had done it before in a yacht of his uncle's, in twenty hours. If the yacht left in the morning it could be home early on Sunday, with or without him, according to what message came through.

'Is there a radio on this boat?' he asked Jamie. 'A ship-to-shore, I mean?'

'It's full o' gadgets, lad. I daresay.'

They surely wouldn't throw him in without knocking him on the head first? He could swim for hours. Jonathan shivered violently.

'You cold? There's a sweater here you can use.'

'Thanks. '

Jamie flung it at him and he pulled it on. Don't think about it. Mummy and Daddy will pay.

Paul's voice came down the hatch. 'Jamie, it's about time.'

Jamie grunted. There was a pause, sound of water-pump being used, glass of water being put on table.

'You've got to take these,' Jamie said. 'Seasick pills.'

'I'm not feeling sick.'

'All the same . . . the boss says.'

Jonathan cottoned on, despair and anger rousing him. 'Look, I'm not simple. Like hell they're seasick pills!—'

'It'll be easier—'

'Why should I make it easy? I didn't want to bloody come, did I?' It would be his only chance, in Breskens, to attract some attention and he didn't intend to miss it. Jamie couldn't force the wretched things down. Could he? Jonathan was fed up with co-operating. Jamie said, cajolingly, 'Come on, it'll be better for you.'

Jonathan held out his hand and Jamie shook three or four tablets into it out of a bottle. Jonathan lunged out hopefully and had the satisfaction of hearing the bottle fly through the air and hit something hard, tablets raining in all directions. So far so good.

'Oh, cripes, you little bastard!' Jamie lamented. 'You're just making it awkward.'

Jonathan knew that picking them up off the floor wasn't going to improve Jamie's queasiness. However, he only needed a few. The next time he handed them Jonathan kicked him, and had a lucky connection, Jamie letting out a howl and much blasphemy.

'You having trouble, Jamie?' a voice called down the hatch.

'Yes, sir. We're not achievin' much at the moment. I think I shall want some help.'

'We're rather busy up here—'

Shrill whirrings of sheet winches confirmed his last remark, with a sharp alteration of heel below as the yacht went about. Jamie lost his balance and crashed his head against the coachroof, judging by the satisfactory noise of bone against wood, and Jonathan, encouraged, wedged himself aggressively with his back against the bulkhead. He might be making life uncomfortable for himself, but not dangerously so, he judged, and it was worth it if it upset the boys upstairs.

'I can't do it on me own, sir,' Jamie called out plaintively. 'You'll have to give me a hand.'

'The finishing line's just coming up. Hang on!'

And a quieter, worried remark from Paul: 'We should have started on him earlier. We'll be in in ten minutes.'

'Blast it! We can lose a bit of time outside if we must.'

'Watch it, Ringo!'

'We're on port tack, idiot. *Jago* will have to free off.'

Jonathan realized that another yacht was in the vicinity

and let out the scream of a lifetime, calculated to reach shore. *Jago* belonged to a friend of his father's called Montgomery Sinclair. He lunged for where he thought the hatch was, successfully caught the companionway ladder and bawled up into the wind, 'Monty! Monty! It's Jonathan Meredith!' and screamed blue murder.

Action was swift and decisive from the deck, a hand crashing into his mouth and his fingers stamped on. He bit the hand fiercely, but was defeated by an attack from below by Jamie which made him scream without any thought for Montgomery Sinclair at all. He'd really started a fight now, with John and Paul descending in panic and Ringo left on the helm bawling, 'For cripes' sake, what about a crew then?' and sounds of sheets running out and sails flapping violently. Jonathan heard a finishing gun, but who for he could not tell. A knell for himself was his last coherent thought, before the three of them set on him at once. He resisted, because he knew Ringo had his hands full on his own and if the yacht was behaving strangely it was all to his advantage, attracting attention, but it was only a matter of stretching time out rather than with any hope of winning. With righteous rage on one's side, surprising strength was summoned—at least, he surprised himself, and perhaps John, by the force of his blind flailing, but eventually they got him down and almost stifled him to death with a cushion while Jamie gathered up the pills and Paul knelt on him, painfully.

'Come on, pack it in! You're only making it worse for yourself.'

But as they wanted him to open his mouth he obliged and screamed again, and John put the cushion back, swearing, and Ringo shouted down, 'For cripes' sake, what shall I do? We can't go in with that row going on!'

'Stand off then,' John bawled back, and got a hold of Jonathan's hair and banged his head several times on the floor. Jonathan didn't like it, although the horse bandage saved him from damage. He opened his mouth to complain and someone stuck a spoon in it and wedged it open. He took the opportunity to scream some more, but they dropped the pills in, followed by a dollop out of the water glass and held his nose, until he had to swallow or burst. God, no wonder the cat fought when they gave it worm pills! Jonathan groaned.

Jamie said in an awed voice, 'You gave him six, sir!'

'I'd give him flaming twelve and do him in if I'd any sense,' John said furiously.

Paul got to his feet, much to Jonathan's relief. 'Better see what Ringo's up to. Halfway to Antwerp by now.'

'See to him, Jamie. Put the cushion on his head and sit on it if he screams again. He'll be out cold in ten minutes.'

Jonathan did, in fact, feel as if nothing mattered very much any more. He couldn't really remember what he'd been making all the fuss about. Jamie told him to sit up. His voice, considering everything, was quite kindly again.

'You shouldn't have done that, lad. It didn't help at all. Just you move into the forepeak now, and get into the bunk up for'ard, and you can have a nice sleep. Give us all a rest.'

He pushed Jonathan in the desired direction and Jonathan went, unaccountably tired. He flopped down onto the bunk and shortly afterwards a large damp foresail was pushed down the hatch above him and gradually, fold by fold, covered him up. Anyone looking into the fo'c'sle wouldn't have known anyone was there at all.

5

Jessica woke early but, remembering, was immediately ashamed that she had slept at all.

'Ugh,' she said out loud, sitting up in bed and scowling at her room. It was going to be another horrible day, with her parents wrapped up in their dilemma and ordinary life suspended indefinitely.

Since Jonathan's disappearance, Jessica had been needled by some difficult emotions. Rather than concern for her brother, she had felt an overwhelming joy and relief that the kidnappers had taken him and not herself, and she found this basic feeling of comfort a great embarrassment. She was ashamed of her natural feelings, but could not change them. In a way it upset her more than what had happened; it made her feel muddled and inadequate, so that waking up on Saturday morning gave her no joy at all. She lay in bed thinking of the great gloom that had fallen over the household, what she thought of as 'the black cloud'. She tried to feel desperately sorry for Jonathan but, having little imagination, it was hard to feel sorry for a condition she knew nothing about and found hard to picture. Apart from which, she had always thought Jonathan entirely capable of handling anything that came his way. He was three years older than her, and aloof and independent, and she never thought of him as a child any more, although her mother had called him a child when she had been talking to the police inspector. She had said, 'For heaven's sake, the child's life is more important than the money!' in a voice of surprising passion. Jessica had got the impression lately that her mother didn't much care for Jonathan, but she certainly wasn't behaving like it now.

Jessica realized, not with pride, that she felt angry with Jonathan rather than sorry for him. The silly business ruined everything. She had been going to go to a horse show to jump Cuthbert and Peter would be there on Sirius and it would have been one of the rare occasions when she would have had a chance to talk to him on her own, without Jonathan there, but now her mother wouldn't leave home to drive the horsebox, and it was too far to hack. Was it too selfish to wonder if the McNairs would pick Cuthbert up in their box? Jessica considered it. After all, there was no point her staying at home being miserable. It didn't help anything. It wouldn't help Jonathan.

She slipped out of bed and put on her dressing-gown, a flouncy very un-Marks and Spencer affair which her father had brought her back from America, and padded silently down the carpeted corridor to the top of the stairs. Their house was very old and crooked in a familiar way: one adjusted to the slopes and avoided the creaks and invariably ducked at danger spots. The beautiful carved oak Jacobean staircase leading down to the square hall below with its polished oak floor floating Eastern rugs of smoky, shimmering colours reminded her—because of Jonathan—that this great privilege of being rich, although it provided ponies and nice clothes and super holidays and plushy schools, was an awful bore when it came to not setting off the burglar alarm late at night, and remembering never to leave the tack-shed unlocked, and making sure that Marcus, the terrier with the loudest bark, was always locked in the sitting-room at bedtime where the Van Gogh was, and now—making sure that ordinary men like plumbers weren't kidnappers . . . Jessica, having taken life for granted ever since she was old enough to

41

think, was shaken by the turn of events. But, even so, she didn't see why she shouldn't go to the horse show.

She went into her father's study and rang the McNairs and asked for Peter. He was ages coming.

'Were you still in bed?'

'Yes.'

Jessica was surprised, for the McNairs got up at dawn, she always thought.

'I was just wondering . . . um . . . it's Jessica—'

'I know.'

'Whether you are taking Sirius to Pond Green show today?'

'No, I'm not.'

'Oh, I thought you were.'

'Yes, I were, but now, owing to indisposition, I am not.'

'Indisposition? Indisposition of what?'

'Indisposition of the foot. No foot, no horse, you know.'

'Sirius is lame?'

'No, I am. Lame unto death.'

'Why? What have you done?'

'Sprained the fetlock.'

'How?'

'Falling off.'

'Oh, how stupid. I was hoping you might give me a lift.'

'Lucky I wasn't expecting sympathy. Any news of brother Jonathan?'

'No.'

'Talking of sympathy, you hard, foul female, you're going to a horse show while the—'

'Well, I can't *do* anything, can I? If you knew what it was like here, you'd understand that getting away for the day is a good idea.'

'Point taken. Sorry about the transport then.'

'It doesn't matter.'

Jessica rang off, disappointed. She turned away from the desk but almost immediately the telephone rang again. Thinking it might be Peter again, she lifted the receiver and said, 'Hullo.'

'Mrs Meredith?' a voice said.

'No, *Miss* Meredith. Jessica.'

'Can you take a message?'

'Yes.' Jessica reached for a handy pencil. 'Fire away.'

'If you want Jonathan Meredith back, the person concerned wants the money delivered tonight. I will give the instructions about delivering it, which you must get quite right. Are you ready?'

Jessica's mouth dropped open.

'Oh, golly, you're the kidnapper. Wouldn't you rather speak to my mother?'

'No, not at all. Don't go away. Have you got a pencil?'

'Yes.'

'It's to be delivered in used twenty-pound notes to a person who will be at Three Ashes crossroads on the Hanningham road at midnight tonight. It's to be delivered by the boy who was with Jonathan Meredith when he was taken, and he is to be alone, on foot, without any sort of escort, and with no police lurking in the vicinity. No harm will come to him. Have you got that?'

'Tonight?'

'Yes.'

'Three Ashes at midnight?'

'That's right. And you must tell your parents—this is very important—that they have only this one chance to deliver the money. If our contact doesn't receive it safely, Jonathan Meredith will not be alive in the morning.'

'You pig,' Jessica said.

The man laughed. 'You're sure you've got that right? Repeat it to me.'

'Three Ashes at midnight, to be delivered by Peter, on foot, in used twenty-pound notes, and if not Jonathan will not be alive in the morning. What are you going to do to him?'

'Not me. I'm only a giver of messages.'

'It's very wrong of you,' Jessica said passionately. 'He hasn't done you any harm. He's *nice*—you shouldn't do it this way, even if you want the money. There's lots of other ways.'

'Goodbye, dear.'

The man rang off, and Jessica was left with the silent receiver in her hand, shocked and horrified. Peter couldn't go on foot—she had just been going to say, after her homily about their ethics. She jiggled the receiver rest up and down, but it only burred obligingly, waiting for her to ring a new number. Horrors! She had made a real mess of it. She took her scribbled notes and ran upstairs, shouting, 'Mummy! Daddy! They rang up!'

After that, the day was horrible, just like the day before, with her parents wrapped in their problem, grey-faced and tense. The police came, and the message was played back—the telephone had apparently been linked to a tape-recorder, and the fatuous conversation with Peter about going to the horse show was also played, which made Jessica blush. Her father was very stern with the police inspector.

'I intend to obey this message, whatever your advice. You do understand that? I happen to believe them when they say we are only going to have the one chance.'

'I'm not going to dissuade you, Mr Meredith. We are in a very difficult position, with absolutely no clue at all as to the boy's whereabouts—not a sniff of the vehicle, no lead from the messages. Nothing to go on at all, in short.

A very baffling situation altogether. I'm in no position to help you, the way things stand at the moment.'

'Well, that's frank, but I appreciate it. The only thing we can hope is that we can trace them afterwards, with information from Jonathan—assuming it all turns out according to plan. Now I suppose I must spend the rest of the day sorting out the cash.'

'And we'll go over to the McNairs',' Mrs Meredith decided. 'I'm sure I don't know why Peter has to be involved in this way. Any one of us could have taken the cash.'

'I take it they feel safer confronting a juvenile,' the inspector said.

Jessica stored up the satisfactory word 'juvenile' as a description of Peter, and asked to accompany the McNair expedition. Her wish granted, she was shortly contemplating Peter's ankle, along with her mother, Mr and Mrs McNair and the police contingent. It was propped up on the sofa, bare and discoloured and very swollen.

'He's hardly going to get up there on that,' Mr McNair said shortly, the situation having been explained. 'Not on foot. In a car, perhaps.'

'I think that would defeat the whole object of the exercise,' Mrs Meredith said firmly. 'He can't drive himself, and I think they want nobody there but Peter. He must be alone. It was one of the conditions.'

'I can go on a horse,' Peter said.

Mrs Meredith's face brightened instantly. 'What an excellent idea! That would fit the bill perfectly.'

Only she and Peter seemed to think it a good idea. The police looked very gloomy; Inspector Marshall stood stroking his chin doubtfully, and Mr McNair looked nervous.

'It's dangerous,' he said.

'Good God, Arthur!' said Mrs Meredith sharply. 'It's nothing to what you have the boy doing every day!'

Mr McNair looked positively embarrassed. His lined, aggressive face turned away and contemplated Peter on the sofa, and Jessica saw that it was the kidnappers he was afraid of, and didn't want to say.

Mrs Meredith said rather snappishly, 'I can't see what on earth you're afraid of, Arthur. They said the boy wouldn't come to any harm. Why on earth should he? He'll have the money and I'm sure Inspector Marshall will agree not to interfere in any way.' She fixed the inspector with a challenging eye.

'We're not intending to alter the course of events, no. I think it would be very dangerous at this stage.'

'How much money am I to take?' Peter asked.

'Five hundred thousand pounds.'

'Cripes! Half a million! How do I take that? I shall want a pack-horse.'

'It will go into a rucksack easily enough,' the inspector said. He looked rather happier about the idea, having considered it. Jessica, thinking about the money, wondered if they were going to be very poor after they had paid for Jonathan. It was an unpleasant thought on top of all the other unpleasant thoughts, and made her feel very uneasy, and guilty again, for thinking it mattered. They might have to sell the ponies! She tried to think about being glad if Jonathan was rescued, but the thought of selling Cuthbert made her want to cry. Jonathan didn't seem to matter nearly so much by comparison. She stared at the carpet, reddening with guilt and dismay. Everything she thought of was wrong, somehow. She felt a very poor specimen of the noble human race.

Police and parents retired to discuss tactics, and Jessica stayed to talk to Peter about the kidnapper ringing up.

She sat beside his foot and stared at it and said, 'I wonder how much money my father has got?'

'Oh, stacks, I reckon.' Peter was very taken with the idea of going for a ride with half a million pounds in cash for company. 'I could ride away into the blue and never come back.'

'Then Jonathan wouldn't come back either.'

'No. Do you think they really mean it then? Is that what he said? Just the one chance?'

'Yes, only tonight. Else he won't be alive tomorrow morning—that's what the man said.'

Peter was awed by his responsibility. Jonathan, the poor twit—did he know how close he was to snuffing it, or was he merely locked up somewhere in blissful ignorance? Jessica, white-faced and with violet shadows under her eyes, looked as if she was suffering, but Peter guessed she was suffering more from atmosphere than actual grief. As if to confirm his thoughts, she said miserably, 'You know, even if he does come back all right, I think everything is going to be awful for a bit.'

'How so? Great rejoicings all round, I would have said.'

'Well, you know what they're like . . . I mean, it's not actually losing the money, but being—well—sort of beaten, I suppose.'

'Held to ransom. Having to do what someone else wants, for a change.'

'Yes. I'm sure they won't just forget it. I think it's going to be horrid.'

Peter thought she was very likely right, and was surprised by her astuteness. The Merediths were tough all right, and most assuredly not used to being ordered around.

'I bet, when they get over being glad to see Jonathan, they'll be cross with him,' Jessica said.

Peter looked at her carefully, interested in the Meredith undercurrents being revealed. 'In that case, I shall defend him. Nobody could ever have guessed—the plumber's van, I mean.'

'He ought to try and escape.'

Peter said scathingly, 'They aren't potty, you know. He'll be tied up and blindfolded and quite likely drugged.'

Jessica burst into tears, still more for Cuthbert than Jonathan in spite of the plight Peter described, and Peter sighed heavily and wished he could move, but couldn't. At least the sight of Jessica's tears wasn't as unnerving as the glint of dew in mother Meredith's hawkish winkers; he made soothing noises and said, 'I'm sure it'll work out all right, really.'

He wasn't at all, really, especially when the police started briefing him for his part in the saga, for which instruction dragged on more or less all day, until it was nearly time for him to depart. Peter tried to look intelligent, but found that the general nervous tension was catching, and his immobility prevented him from keeping out of the way. It was all people coming and going and telling him things. They bandaged up his ankle and the money arrived in a solidly-packed rucksack which he tried for size and weight and found perfectly accommodating, if awesome. He insisted on using Sirius, his own pony, and his father said Sirius wasn't suitable; and Mrs Meredith told him not to be ridiculous again, and went home to fetch a stirrup-light. The day drew in to a short, cold evening, very dark. Peter hopped outside to avoid the general company; he felt pressed and irritable, anxious to be away, nervous of his responsibilities towards Jonathan. He felt deeply concerned for Jonathan's life, for the first time, his own part in the business looming distinctly vital to Jonathan's well-being. What if nobody turned up to meet him? Why him anyway? Oh, Jonathan . . . optimism waned as the night sky closed like a blindfold over the cold horizons, shutting out the familiar fields and lines of yellowing elms, bringing the smell of rain and the chill of fear. It didn't do to court solitude; he struggled back indoors to the comfort of the anguished Merediths and the tight-lipped, edgy police. There was a strange companionship threaded into the general gloom; the atmosphere was extraordinary: tense and bare and elemental and nothing like the general Meredith drinks-before-dinner to which Peter was accustomed: no small talk, no trivia, but just the stark faces with eyes watching the clock, and the communal concern. Peter retreated into the kitchen to eat some supper; the police were on cheese sandwiches and the Merediths on whisky. Peter was glad when it was time to go, although by then it was raining intermittently and there was a strong wind up. They fetched him a jersey and anorak and his bad foot was fitted into a large plimsol; he was then given two strong shoulders for support and conveyed out into the stable-yard, where his father had Sirius ready, who was looking understandably amazed at being disturbed from his peace in the middle of the night. Mrs Meredith bunked him up, and the rucksack was handed up, the stirrup-light adjusted, his watch synchronized. It was all extremely odd. Peter crammed his hat down firmly and picked up the reins.

'Well—' There wasn't anything to say, really.

The Merediths gave him bleak smiles of encouragement.

'Be careful,' his father said severely, and Peter eased Sirius from his impatient halt and moved away down the drive, thankful to be moving at last. The pony—a Wembley showjumper and a temperamental beast at the best of times—walked sideways, arching his neck with exaggerated delicacy, and Peter knew that if the animal played up he was going to miss his duff leg. He growled at him and cursed a bit, and Sirius decided that it was for real, and settled down once he was on the road. The rain was coming down steadily, running in the gutters, and the first falling leaves were coming down in the gusts of wind, pale as flakes of snow. Peter huddled down in the saddle, not enchanted with his lot, scowling up into the wet darkness and wriggling his shoulders beneath the weight of half a million pounds. The actual fact of being in possession of that amount of money was harder to credit than anything else; if it bore heavily on his shoulders now, it was as nothing compared with how it was likely to bear on Jonathan's conscience when he came back—if Jessica's prognosis was anything to go by. It was a colossal amount to lose; whether it was likely to affect the Meredith lifestyle Peter had no way of knowing.

Late Saturday night traffic flashed past occasionally, too close for comfort—inebriated probably, Peter thought—but when he turned off on to the Three Ashes lane it was deathly quiet, stirring only to the gurgling of rainwater in the ditches and the rustle of rabbit and pigeon. Peter, solemn and uneasy, watched the wet flick of the pony's ears and the dark hole of the lane between high thick hedges. It climbed steadily uphill, and the water ran down in gravelly channels, awakening the clammy smells of the season's end, of turned earth and trampled leaves. Two weeks ago it had still been dusty stubble. Sirius walked out freely—probably too freely: glancing at his luminous watch, Peter knew he would be early. He would have to wait. He wished he knew what for—a car? It was going to be creepy; he could feel it getting creepy already, thinking ahead, listening to the soft creaking of the trees overhead in the wind, eerie, unpredictable. The sky was wet and wild and black, but the high hedges sheltered him; the rain came broken, in fits and starts.

The rendezvous stipulated by the man on the telephone was a crossing of two lanes on the top of a hill. The landscape opened out and the high banks and hedges fell away, leaving only a few exposed and half-dead elms between Peter and the elements. He reached the crossroads a quarter of an hour before time, and swore to himself, cold now, and his ankle throbbing painfully, and feeling distinctly nervous. Sirius, pulled up, put his tail to the wind and fidgeted crossly, not used to standing about at the best of times, and Peter let him graze to settle him. There was no sign of life at all, only the spasmodic gleam of a headlight on a road some two miles away, too far away to be of any comfort or company. The man had chosen well. The lanes were a long way round to nowhere at the best of times, and Peter guessed that the only person he would meet until he got back to the main road would be the mystery man collecting his cool half million.

He waited. The rain splattered in fitful gusts on the back of his anorak and trickled uncomfortably down his neck and over his knees. His watch-hand crept to midnight. Nothing happened. He walked Sirius about, up and down, to keep themselves warm, but no car came; the soft squelching of Sirius's hooves in the grass was the only sound. The rain ran in black lines down the pony's flanks, began to stick Peter's clothes to his body in clammy patches, only the money keeping his spine warm. He began to wonder if he had come to the right place, or if Jessica had heard right, whether something was amiss that he couldn't know about. He stopped being frightened, irritation and pure misery taking over instead. He had anticipated all sorts of possibilities in his meeting with the kidnapper, but he had never considered that it might be a non-event. The anti-climax was worse than anything. And what of Jonathan . . . did it mean that something had gone wrong? Perhaps he was already dead, or perhaps he had escaped? The uncertainty needled Peter; it was worse than anything. Surely the police hadn't waylaid the person he was waiting for, not after their assurances? He looked at his watch again. Coming up to half-past midnight. Give it five minutes, he thought, and then I'll find a phone-box and call the police for advice.

Sirius, grazing, put up his head suddenly and stiffened. Peter instinctively stiffened too, listened and heard nothing. His pulses thumped unpleasantly.

'What is it, Sirius idiot?' he murmured, more to reassure himself than the pony.

He listened again.

Nothing.

The pony turned his head and gazed away sideways, not down the lane at all, but across the field. Quite suddenly he whinnied.

Oh, cripes, Peter thought, something is going to happen!

He heard it then, not what he expected at all. The tight, thumping fear came back again. He gathered up his reins and turned Sirius sharply to face the approaching sound.

6

It seemed to take a lifetime to work out what was happening, to remember where he was. Even when he had worked it out, Jonathan found it hard to believe, and felt too ill to care anyway. He lay inside his black cocoon, shivering, gritting his teeth to make himself bear it, not wanting to die but feeling that it could only be a happy release to his present suffering.

No sound of human endeavour from any quarter, only the buffeting of water on the yacht's hull. She was sailing fast, close-hauled, and the forward berth was abominably uncomfortable, the bows pitching and screwing through the hostile ocean, dropping into troughs like a falling stone. Jonathan, braced hard by his knees against the bunkboard, preferred unconsciousness, but could not summon it back. He knew he would be sick if he did not escape to less extreme quarters, but it took even more will-power to sit up and move than it did to go on lying there, the change of equilibrium proving distinctly unpleasant. He heard himself groaning, but didn't care, feeling his way past the bulkhead and into the saloon. Still no sounds of life, and he started to undo the blindfold, but he had only got it half off when a voice close at hand said, 'Stop that, you perisher, or we'll do you a violence.'

Someone firmly did it up again, and Jonathan didn't feel like another argument. He was too weak.

'Can't I go on deck? It's ghastly down here. I shall be sick all over everything and you'll have to clear it up.'

'Yeah, I wouldn't be surprised. I'm still clearing up after Jamie.'

'It's those lousy pills.'

'Not with Jamie it isn't. He's a natural.'

'Cripes, if I don't get some fresh air I shall—' Jonathan felt desperate. He thought he was going to pass out, feeling everything going round and round—or, at least, if he could have seen anything it felt as if it would be going round and round: the blindfold made it all twice as bad. 'Please—I must go on deck. I won't do anything—'

'Okay. You'll need oilskins. Hang on a minute.'

It was Ringo, the more helpful of his adversaries . . . he found Jonathan a heavy jersey and the oilskins, which Jonathan struggled into, and then guided him out through the hatch. The cold wind caught Jonathan's face, drenching him with spray. It was magnificent after the clammy stench of old cooking, vomit, and diesel fuel below and Jonathan drank it in gratefully, grasping the cockpit coamings and bracing himself to the acute angle of heel. Water was coming aboard in big dollops. Ringo passed him a towel to fold round his neck and Jonathan pulled his hood up and fastened up the lacings of the oilskin top.

'If you get into that corner on the bridgedeck you'll be out of the way.' John's voice, from the tiller, sounded quite amiable. 'We shan't be tacking for an hour or so.'

'Where are we?'

'Homeward bound.'

'Is it dark?' Funny, but even inside the blindfold he sensed that it was night-time.

'Too right. Black as your hat.'

Could it still be Friday night? Jonathan had lost track, even after thinking about it hard. There was a lost dimension somewhere.

'Saturday night?'

54

He surely couldn't have lost that much time . . .?

'Yeah. Twenty-three thirty hours exactly.'

Cripes, no wonder he felt so lost out—he had been unconscious for over twenty-four hours! His head was thumping like a steam-hammer. He was freezing cold yet had a curious sensation as if of sweating, and his mouth was dry as old toast. He also still had the feeling of being suffocated, a desperate stifled sensation which he put down to being blindfolded for so long.

'Look—if it's so dark—it wouldn't matter, would it, if I had this thing off—it makes me feel awful—'

Ringo's voice said, 'It wouldn't matter to me. I'm turning in for a few hours. Better ask the boss.'

'You go below,' John said to Ringo. 'I'll call you if I want you. We'll want the wireless on about one, remember. It'll be all hands then.' His voice then turned to Jonathan and, to his infinite relief, said, 'Okay, Meredith, you can take it off, but keep your eyes front. No funny business.'

The relief was fantastic, a rebirth into the real world, the darkness not one wit as dark as he had been suffering for two whole days: but grey and close and real and beautiful. Jonathan's eyes, released, took in the glimmering, shiny-wet cabin-top and the spray-dark sails, closely reefed, and foaming decks curtsying to the water. The yacht was a beauty, carving a wet, sleek passage into the night: not a light showed in any direction, not a single star, the heavy clouds showing merely darker in the whole darkness. Jonathan lifted his face to the wind and felt the blessed cold on his eyeballs, the tears coming at the shock of it. It was beautiful, in spite of everything. He shifted himself to comfort, locking his fingers over the coaming and resting his chin there, watching the water running in continuous streams down the pitching deck. Pale marblings of foam heaved in their wake. The spray beat on his face and crackled on the gleaming oilskins. The smell was of oceans a thousand fathoms deep: no exaggeration could possibly cover all the extremes of his feeling, it was so crystal perfect, the strength and the freedom of the boat sailing through the black night.

It was only then, slowly and painfully, that he remembered the significance of what John had just said, about putting the wireless on at one o'clock. If the money was not forthcoming and a message came through to say so, he was to be put over the side. This would happen, presumably, in a bare two hours' time, so that this sudden and loving awareness of cleaving so splendidly through the North Sea was quite likely to be his last impression of living. The realization came almost gently; not with a sudden shock, but with a creeping, quiet recollection. He did not move, but went on staring at the water—amazed, in fact, that he could contemplate his imminent death with such calm, and then not amazed at all, for what other course could win him a reprieve? It was a fact of life, this likelihood of death, and to shout and scream would not alter it. The message would decide. He must wait two hours for the message, and he must not show his fear. It was a matter of self-respect. He felt he had a good deal to make up when it came to self-respect. Nobody on board knew in fact that he had heard about his likely fate; if his likely fate overtook him, nobody would ever know that he had had two hours to consider it in. All this went through his head quite slowly, heavily, leaving him with a slightly breathless sensation at the enormity of it. It wasn't easy to accept, to put it mildly. It had to be given time. The water which he had been admiring so ardently a few minutes before, now took on a far more sinister significance. Jonathan didn't like it, and turned round, straightening up.

'Keep your eyes front,' John said sharply.

Jonathan obeyed. He moved more central and turned his gaze on the sails instead. He guessed there would be a number on the mainsail, but it was too dark to read it.

'Have you ever helmed a boat like this?' John asked him.

'Yes.'

'Come and take the tiller then, while I have a look at the chart. The course is three one zero, if you can hold it. It's okay at the moment, and with luck—according to the weather forecast—will improve.'

Jonathan moved back, surprised at the command, but glad of it. Fifty-odd hours of doing nothing at all was surprisingly tiring, and he wanted something to think about, other than the obvious. The compass was illuminated by a tiny glow of light. Jonathan watched it, reaching for the tiller.

'Okay?'

'Yes.'

John stood in the hatch for a little while, to make sure. He was a medium-sized figure in oilskins, impossible to see any more. Very little of his face showed beneath sou'wester and turned-up collar, and a swathe of towel, not enough to ascertain any features. Jonathan, after a glance, turned his eyes on the compass and kept them there, until John disappeared below. The tiller kicked in his hand and he braced his legs across the cockpit; the feeling of power was impressive. Strange, to feel enjoyment in this at the same time as waiting to be murdered: it was so strange, in fact, that the mind would not accept it. It just wanted to enjoy the sailing and blank out about the future. Jonathan went along with his instincts, ducking his head against the flying spray and watching his course. The yacht was magnificent and so was the wild dark sea pulling against his arm, and that was enough.

57

John wedged himself in the hatch, having checked the log, made his dead reckoning and satisfied himself on their position. He passed Jonathan up a cheese sandwich and then a cup of tea.

'What's the time?' Jonathan asked.

'Twenty past midnight.' Not long, Jonathan thought. And then, they *wouldn't* . . .!

'Okay?' John asked.

'Yes.'

How could one be convinced that his parents would pay up? They were both fighters by nature, not easily dictated to. No harm in asking.

'This plan of yours—what happens when we get back?'

'It depends whether we've got what we asked for.'

'How will you know?'

'There's a message coming through on the ship-to-shore between one and two o'clock.' He glanced at his watch. 'Shortly, with luck.'

'To say if my parents have paid up?'

'That's right.'

'If they have, you let me go?'

'Yeah, that's the bargain. They get you back.'

'And if they haven't—?'

John hesitated. Then he said softly, 'Let's not talk about it. They'll pay, the way we've put it to them.'

Jonathan wished he hadn't asked. John's voice suggested sympathy, which was ominous.

John said, 'There's plenty of time.' Time for chucking him in, Jonathan supposed, before they came to the shipping lanes out of the Thames estuary. A sharp burst of rain came like artillery, pelleting down the taut mainsail. John pulled the hatch closer to and said, 'If you want a spell, I'll call Ringo up.'

'No.' Jonathan shrugged down inside his clothes as

the rain bit in, creeping towards his cold collar-bones. The compass light glowed with its soft familiarity, the needle ranging uneasily. There was a loom on the horizon to the south, very faint between the showers.

'The West Hinder,' John said. 'She's going well. If you're happy then, I'll go down and tune in to Channel sixteen.'

'Yes.'

He was cold, but he didn't want anything else. Cold and wet and stupid and frightened for his life, but he didn't want to be taken off the tiller. Alone in the cockpit, he thought that this, paradoxically, was the best thing he had ever done in his life. The rain eased off but the sky was darker than ever, as dark as the sea, but without the paler lacings of blown spume. He could hold his course without difficulty. The West Hinder faded gradually and disappeared for good below the horizon. Jonathan sat on and nobody looked out from below or came to say anything to him. He could see one solitary star between clouds, and its unwinking eye transfixed him with this extraordinary sense of his own being, because he shortly wouldn't be. He had to stand up, because the feeling wouldn't be contained sitting down; he had to rise to this mind-bending conception of whatever it was he was facing. It was perhaps something of the same feeling said to be experienced during a long fall—the recollection of one's life in a few seconds—yet in Jonathan's case it was the same intense perception in a more abstract form, not in the form of being aware of people and past happenings, but in being aware of the present, with what amounted almost to violence. He was trembling, perhaps with cold. He didn't think so. He fixed his eyes on the compass to steady the threat of hysteria, then it was all right. And the star—the steadiness of the star soothed him.

He did not know how long he was in the cockpit alone, but later John came up, and then Ringo. Jonathan realized they were there, rather than saw them emerge. He asked the time.

'It's half-past two,' John said.

'Has the message come through?' Jonathan asked.

'No.'

Nobody said anything else. Ringo checked the course and sat on the opposite side of the cockpit with John, behind Jonathan. Jonathan was aware of them, without being able to see them. They didn't offer to take him off the helm, which he would have resisted. He could sense the heaviness of their spirits. He felt very clear-headed now. He knew that he would not be capable of resisting the four of them when they decided to put him over; it was merely a matter of waiting for them to broach the moment. He knew that they would have to—there was no way out for them—yet he knew they didn't want to. In a strange way he felt stronger, more capable, than he thought they did. He was intoxicated, keyed up to this quivering pitch of life awareness. He wanted to hold on to it, for the contemplation of actually drowning was something he could not face. He would not think about it for he knew that it would do for him. The horrors were a hairsbreadth away, and he was on a tightrope high above the black pit, his being fastened on a star. But the star had gone.

'What's the time?' John asked Ringo.

'Twenty to three.' There was a long pause and then, 'What do you think?'

Another long pause. 'We'll give it till three. Then that's it. No backing down, we all agreed.'

'Okay.'

Jonathan fixed his eyes on the compass. The yacht was holding her course more and more easily, closing with home rapidly. He decided to concentrate on the compass alone, fasten his mind to another constant of the universe, the magnetic north, and not let it deviate, for twenty minutes was a lifetime and he didn't know whether he could hold on.

7

The man had come to collect the money on horseback. Peter found it hard to credit, and was moved to say 'Snap!', but desisted. The moment having arrived, he found it more amusing than frightening. He turned Sirius and went to meet him. The man had come across the fields, and jumped out on to the lane through a thin part of the hedge and over the ditch. Peter noticed that he rode well, and that the horse had been ridden hard, but was fit and a goer. He turned Sirius and rode to meet him.

'You're late,' he said.

The man pulled up and Peter sensed that he was surprised, but it was impossible to discern his expression, his face being hidden by a scarf, a pair of sunglasses, and a bush-hat pulled well down. He wore black oilskins.

'Cripes, are you on a horse too? I can't see a thing through these bloody glasses. I thought they said on foot?' The voice, slightly breathless, was perfectly friendly, in spite of the implied criticism, well-educated and that of a young man. Peter was taking mental notes. It was too dark to see anything useful.

'Yes, but I can't. I've sprained my ankle. I thought you weren't coming.'

'Hmm. Yes. A few unexpected hitches. Let's have it then. I take it we've no spectators? No lurkers in the undergrowth?'

'No. All quite above board. I can't dismount. Can you take it?'

He shrugged out of the straps and the man dismounted and took the rucksack off him. He put it on the ground and opened it up and examined the contents with a torch.

'Cripes,' he said. 'Pure money—no rocks in the bottom . . . not every day one has the privilege of humping half a million. How does it feel?'

He fastened it up and swung it up on to his back.

'Nice,' Peter said. 'Not too heavy, considering . . .'

'The nearest I'll ever come to a fortune.'

He gathered up his reins and mounted the horse again. He was very agile, although of a stocky build. Without the rucksack he would probably have vaulted. Peter didn't know what he had expected, but the exchange was quick and painless and seemed in no way at all to have criminal overtones. The man had no psychopathic characteristics, showed no signs of nervous tension, of guilt, not even of unfriendliness.

'That's it then. Thanks a million.' He laughed at his pun, turned his horse round and kicked it towards the gap where he had jumped before. The horse, wanting to stay with Sirius, refused. The man swore, turned it round and faced it at the hedge again and it refused a second time.

'Bloody hell,' the man said. 'Have you got a whip?'

'No. I'll give you a lead if you like.'

'Okay. Good.'

Peter gathered up his reins and turned Sirius round in a shallow circle to approach the jump, easing him into a canter. Sirius went over with his usual gay abandon and the big horse followed him and went past in a shower of flying mud and clods. The man shouted over his shoulder, 'Thanks! Cheerio!' Something dark flew up from his hand and landed in the grass. Peter pulled Sirius up and walked over to the spot. It was too dark to see very well, but something glinted faintly on the ground. It was the pair of sunglasses. Peter held Sirius still, and looked in the direction the man had gone, but could see nothing. It was downhill and good galloping grass. He could hear the distant thud of hooves, travelling fast, and waited until the sound had faded. Then there was only the soft murmur of thin rain on the grass and on his anorak. It gleamed on the pony's dark shoulders. Peter waited, thinking.

It was clever, he decided. If there had been a reception committee, or police-cars on the road, he could have evaded the lot with no trouble at all. Nobody could follow him the way he'd gone. Only me, Peter thought. He slipped his feet out of the stirrups and crossed the leathers over the front of the saddle. If he was going to ride, his bad ankle felt better hanging free. Then he turned Sirius down the field and put him into a canter. Sirius went eagerly, bored with all the waiting about.

Peter knew the topography well enough and could guess at the man's route, for there was an obvious way for a horse that could jump. Several ways, actually, but with the pocket torch he had been provided with Peter had no doubt he could follow the fresh tracks in the wet ground. If his guess was correct, the man would take a line through a wood known as Pitchy Bottoms, across a defunct railway line and go out across a mile of pastures to a gate on to a road which led directly out to a big arterial. No doubt he had a car waiting there. He could be in it and driving away inside ten minutes, and if anyone had tried to follow him in a car from the meeting-place, they would have been very lucky to beat him to it, for the distance was four times as far by road. Clever, Peter thought admiringly! Full marks for ingenuity. The whole plot had been fiendishly clever up to now, with no smell of Jonathan's hiding-place at all, and not a clue to be found. It was only their bad luck that he had seen the poor lad go, spirited away by a plumber; without his own evidence, Jonathan would have vanished into thin air absolutely, no sight, sound or utterance remaining. Intelligent, A-level crookery, intellectually planned, high-class execution . . . Peter was impressed. But with luck, now, he might capture a clue, i.e., a horse—unless the meeting at the gate was by horse-box—good point. If no horse, telephone to look for horsebox. But not to stop same. The money must get through to save poor Jonathan from his doom. All this went through Peter's head as he galloped down the long hill, holding hard on to Sirius who would happily have attempted a Derby record by the feel of him.

'Idiot!' Peter wasn't in the mood for a fight, feeling tired, and his ankle hurting quite badly. 'The idea isn't to catch him up, brute!' His bad leg was a considerable handicap in getting his own way. He had to use his thigh and knee, and the effort seemed to spread down and concentrate the pain in the part that he thought wasn't doing any work at all. It made him feel a little short-tempered with Sirius.

'For God's sake, *beast*—!' Down by the wood, a little probing with the torch showed the hoofprints going into the trees over a formidable stile, where Peter had anticipated. Peter took Sirius up to it to have a look, not sure about jumping in the dark. He wouldn't have tried it on anything but Sirius. It would have been perfectly acceptable if he had been fit, but the thought of a fall and being stuck miles from nowhere until someone sent out a search party was not attractive. Sirius was not the sort of animal to stay faithfully by his master unto death; he would tear off with his legs all tangled up in the reins and meet certain disaster.

'So behave yourself, animal. This is deadly serious.' Accent on the deadly. He took Sirius away from the stile and turned him round. Sirius, pulling hard, belted for the obstacle in characteristic manner and Peter prayed that the pony could see it better than he could, for the darkness of the wood behind it was total. God, his *leg* . . . ! What I *do* for you, Jonathan! Sirius leapt, beautifully, agonizingly, with miles to spare. A branch knocked Peter's hat down over his eyes, and by the time he could see again Sirius was away down a squelching ride which Peter felt rather than saw, hunched down in the saddle, wincing against the overhanging hawthorn and wild rose twigs which tore at their path. He steadied into a cautious canter, but kept on going, his eyes groping into the darkness until a faint, paler archway indicated the way out through the trees. He thought it was a ditch and rails, but felt bound to pull up and look at it first, in case a strand of wire might have been added. Sirius thought otherwise, and they had a short fight, ending up backside down the ditch and both rather bad-tempered. Peter peered around with his torch, saw the big round hoofprints of his quarry fresh in the soft peat, and the jump innocuous enough to jump almost from a standstill. Out in the open again, Sirius was tearing at the reins, intoxicated by his gallop and the strangeness of working in the dark. The rain streamed off his shoulders and Peter could feel the steam coming off him—or was it himself? He felt exhausted. He swore at Sirius and went searching for the gap up on to the railway embankment, which no doubt was grown over by now—or had the man gone out at the bottom, through the gate? But if he had, it was a longer way round. Peter decided to chance it and go the way he knew was the quickest. He found what looked the thinnest way through and forced a passage up the bank, feeling Sirius hit the nice firmness of railway clinker, a pleasant change from mud. The rails had been taken up and the old route made a curving tunnel through tall, creaking elm. The leaves were coming down like confetti. Peter pushed Sirius on, eager to see if his deductions were correct. Detective-Inspector McNair . . .

searching for clues . . . he fancied the role, but wished the pony was a bit more amenable. 'Constable Sirius, *obedience*, if you please! Do as—you're—bloody well told—' The pony napped at the opening down into the far field, shying at a fallen tree-trunk half across his path and nearly unseating Peter in his stirrupless state. Peter swore again, wanting two good legs badly and having to achieve by guile what he could have done so much more efficiently with a normal pair of working limbs. Sirius a year ago had been earmarked for the knacker's for his intractability, and was never likely to be anything but a difficult ride, but Peter was bored by docility. At times like this he would have preferred it, but the choice had been his own and useless now to complain.

He halted at the edge of the big grass fields to listen, but could hear no signs of life apart from their own heavy breathing. He could find no more hoofmarks, but decided to make for the road and examine the gates that gave on to it. There were only two, as far as he remembered, about a mile away. He knew he had made good time and hoped the man he was trailing had made better, for his intention was not to catch him up. All the same, he went into a steady canter, and Sirius covered the ground rapidly, still pulling, his hooves throwing up squelchy clods behind. Nearer the road Peter steadied, wanting to listen, but there was still nothing to be heard. He wondered if he was completely up the creek with his clever thinking . . . what a sell . . .

'Steady on, beast. Let me get the torch out—'

The first gate was closed and showed no signs of hoofmarks or footprints. It was also padlocked. Peter swore some more, and jumped it, clattering out on to the tarmac. No luck. If the other gate was as virgin all he would have for his clever thinking was a very long ride home and a pretty stupid story to tell. Disheartened, he turned Sirius up the road towards the second gate. Sirius walked on eagerly, but kept pricking his ears up and gazing over the hedge as if he could hear something. Another horse, Peter guessed, and pulled up. Cripes, he had surely not overtaken the bloke with the money? For a moment he sat still, listening to his own heart thumping with apprehension. Then Sirius let out a whinny, and an answering whinny came back from over the hedge, followed in a few moments by the squelching of hooves. From the spasmodic rhythm Peter knew the horse was loose, not ridden.

'And thank Heaven for that!' he murmured fervently, still tingling with the fright of thinking he had messed the whole thing up. 'Ugh!' He was all clammy with rain and the hot sweat of fear.

'And we're right after all, Sirius, by the look of it.'

The horse the man had ridden was right beside them on the other side of the hedge, its neck white with lather. It had been stripped of its tack, and was walking on its toes keeping up with Sirius, excited, blowing out through distended nostrils. Peter examined the grass by the other gate, saw where the horse had been pulled up, making long streamers of mud in the torn grass, saw footprints on both sides of the gate and the tyre-marks of a car on the verge. He kept Sirius on the tarmac so as not to disturb them and sat there for a moment to enjoy the uncommon glow of self-satisfaction. Detective-Inspector McNair had won through.

'We're bloody bright, Sirius, whatever they say.'

But after a few moments the glow wore off, and he realized that the nearest telephone box was at least another mile away, and the night was by no means over.

'You're *where*?' his father exploded on the other end of the line. 'I've been worried out of my mind! What on earth—'

'Look, it's all right. But you've got to come and pick me up, in the box. Bring another headcollar, a big one. I've got another horse.'

'Are you *raving*?'

'It's a clue, for God's sake. Tell the Inspector to come. There's lots of clues.' He explained where he was and rang off, annoyed by his father's idiot reaction. Anti-climax was setting in fast, especially now he was on the ground. The prospect of remounting was dismal, but the prospect of staying on the ground was worse. He hadn't the nerve to vault, his ankle was hurting so, and went through the probably far more painful process of letting the stirrup down to the last hole and mounting in the orthodox manner, which meant that he had to put all his weight on the agony for a second or two, which left him jibbering. Sirius, sympathetic for once, or perhaps worn out, stood still while he moaned and muttered to himself. Being alone, one could give vent. Riding back to the gate which he had made the rendezvous, he reflected on how much one's behaviour, noble or otherwise, depended on who was watching.

'An interesting point, Sirius, don't you think?'

But hard to come to any conclusions, especially at two o'clock in the morning. He yawned. He was very wet, although the rain was easing off, and getting cold now the excitement was over. The road was deserted, large puddles gleaming. Nobody used it at night. Peter walked Sirius along the white line in the middle, arrived at the gate and waited. The crook's horse, moving restlessly up and down on the other side of the gate, was churning up all the footprints, but there were some nice ones where he couldn't get at them. Peter was content.

The police came first, in two cars, and Peter made sure they didn't pull up on his clues, stationing himself nicely in the way. Detective-Inspector Marshall and his posse got out and Peter explained what had happened and indicated the footsteps and the tyre-marks, which were immediately roped off with official posts and string.

'And the horse is in the field,' Peter said, wondering how they were going to cope with that. 'He abandoned it.'

'Was it stolen, I wonder? This is certainly a new line in getaways.'

'If he did, he knew it could jump. Only a good jumper could have come the way he took.'

'That's interesting. If we identify the horse, we might get a lead. Your father might recognize it.'

'He might. Oh, and another thing—a pair of sunglasses. He threw them off in the grass—but that's up by the meeting-place. I should think they'd be easy enough to find.'

'Good. Let's have your description of the man.'

Peter was giving this when his father arrived in the horsebox, breaking up the official calm with his usual steam and thrust. Marshall dispatched him to catch the horse, which he did, throwing questions back over his shoulder. The gate was padlocked and he couldn't get back.

'I'll go back to the other one—'

'That's locked too,' Peter said.

'You said it could jump,' the Inspector said.

'Well, not on its own,' Peter pointed out. 'They don't.'

'I'd like to take it back and see if we can get it identified. Do you recognize it, Mr McNair?'

'I might if I could see it.'

'We'll have to send down to the farm for the key to the padlock. It'll be quicker than filing it. Take the Mini, Andrews—'

'Oh, hang on,' Peter's father broke in. 'We'll be all night. We'll get a bridle on it and Peter can jump it back. Someone come and hold it and I'll sort it out.'

They boxed Sirius and put Sirius's bridle on the horse, having to let out all the holes.

'You want the saddle?' his father asked.

'No, not with this ankle.'

'Here, I'll give you a leg-up.'

'I'll have to jump the hedge, else I'll mess up the marks. Find me an easy bit.'

They obliged, lighting the chosen spot with the car headlamps, and Peter put the horse at it fairly fast. It didn't feel like refusing at all; it was very powerful and keen, a nice beast. It flew the hedge and landed in the middle of the road with a great clatter and sparking of iron shoes and pulled up obediently.

Mr McNair said, 'Seeing it jump, it reminds me of that hunter of Mrs Allsop's. You know the one I mean, Peter? Don't remember what it was called. Came down from Warwickshire two or three winters ago.'

'Could be.' Peter rode it up the ramp of the horsebox and slid off into the straw, reaching for the headcollar that was dangling on a rope from the ring. His one good leg felt terribly tired, almost beyond supporting him, and the Detective-Inspector unexpectedly came up the ramp and helped him out and gave him a shoulder to lean on to the door of the cab.

'You've done a good job of work tonight,' he said. 'The rest of my questions can wait till morning. You go and get some sleep, and we'll get to work on your clues. They might prove very useful. I'll see you tomorrow.'

Peter decided he liked Marshall. He was quiet and patient and kindly, not a bit like his father. His father, getting into the cab and starting up the engine, only said,

'God, boy, I've been sick with worry wondering what you were up to. Let's hope the rest of the night's our own.'

Peter made a face into the darkness, slithered lower into the leather seat and went to sleep.

8

Jonathan, having recovered consciousness, lay without moving for a long time. It was strange how long it took each grain of meaning to penetrate: first, that he could see, next that he was alone and that he appeared to be lying in the open air under some trees and—all the time—how ill he felt.

Having established the scene and the fact that he could look at it, he shut his eyes again. It was better that way. He could not remember what had happened, but he was sure it was very nasty and would give him no joy in the remembering. Why push it? He blanked out his mind and concentrated on breathing. It was not to be taken for granted, but appreciated, and he was quite happy for a while to do just that. It was very quiet, and wet, and the sun was shining somewhere far away, and a bird was singing. He lay in a scrumpled heap, as he had been dropped, but with returned consciousness it gradually began to get very uncomfortable. It was then that he rolled over on to his back and opened his eyes for the second time.

He was in no hurry. In fact, for a long time he wondered how long he could stay away, here in the tranquility of the woods. Going back was going to be awful, he had no doubt about it, as bad as being taken away in the first place. To be questioned and probed, forced to reveal the full extent of his failure—for failure it most certainly had been. It was going to be everything he always made a great point of avoiding in his life—

confrontations with a lot of people he didn't want to know, not to mention confrontations with people he knew a damned sight too well already. He sighed deeply. The sun was coming through the leaves, thin and clear after the heavy rain, and the ground was putting out the steaming scents of long-locked-up humus and animal odour, of peat and roots and droppings and dew. Jonathan could feel the wet grass on his face. He licked his lips, tasting crusty salt, and put his dry mouth to the wetness. It was ice-cold, delicious. The inside of his head felt as if it were on fire, although his body was shivering. He felt very weak and sick and altogether clobbered.

Not dead, though. He tried to accept this fact as a comfort, but it wasn't. He had faced dying quite reasonably well, he considered, in the proper British fashion of stiff upper lip, but afterwards, when the message had come through which meant he wasn't going to die after all—that was a different matter. That was the episode he would prefer to forget. But they would ask him questions and find out. At home they would all find out about his failings, but they would never find out about how he had faced dying. He wouldn't tell them and nobody else knew. Because, in a funny way, facing staying alive had been far worse, and he hadn't been able to cope. When it mattered, at the end, he had gone under. And he was in no hurry to let them all find out.

He felt bad, as bad in the mind as in body, but he couldn't really lie there for ever. Somewhere not too far away he could hear occasional traffic. By the sun it appeared to be late morning, possibly later, and he thought it was still Sunday. If he got to the road, he could work something out.

He got to his feet and stood upright, swaying. He felt as if he was still on the boat, everything going up and down. There was something on the ground, under where he had been lying—the horse bandage that had been used as a blindfold. He knew he should pick it up and take it with him but the inclination not to bend down was so strong that he left it. It was a yellow one and quite conspicuous in the grass; if anyone wanted it they could come and collect it later. He started to walk very slowly towards the sound of traffic, but it was difficult: the ground didn't seem to be where he put his feet, but either higher or lower, so that he seemed to be staggering about like a drunk. Once he fell. He thought it must mean that God meant him to lie down, and didn't get up for a bit, but gradually he came to realize that God didn't really care about his condition at all, and he might as well carry on with trying to get home. The awfulness of going home was not going to abate by putting it off. It never occurred to him that anyone might be pleased to see him.

It seemed to take a long time to get to the road, and when he did it appeared to be a very minor road. There were woods on both sides, unfamiliar to Jonathan. He had no idea where he was at all. He stood there watching the trees going up and down in front of him, and a car came along and pulled up beside him. He stared at it, not aware that he had done anything to cause it to stop, and a woman wound the window down, stuck her head out and said, 'Are there any blackberries in there, do you know?'

'No,' said Jonathan.

'You know any good places?'

Jonathan couldn't even think what a blackberry was. He didn't answer. The woman was fat and tart-looking, fiftyish, wearing a hat and a tweed coat and sensible shoes. She was looking at him sharply.

'Are you all right?' she asked.

'I would like—a lift, as far as a—telephone box.' It seemed to be quite difficult to talk. 'Please,' he added.

The woman turned and said something to the man

driving, presumably her husband, who said, 'Can't do any harm, to a telephone box.' The woman turned in her seat and opened the back door. Jonathan got in and sat down. The plastic seat was warmed by the sun and very comfortable. He made a great effort to shut the door, and to say, 'Thank you,' then he lay back and shut his eyes. It was beautiful.

He felt the car drive on. He couldn't open his eyes. The woman turned round again and said, 'Are you sure you're all right,' and he made another superlative effort and said, 'Yes. Quite all right.' He opened his eyes very wide and stared at her hard to reassure her, but she turned away quickly and started talking to her husband in a soft voice. Jonathan couldn't hear what she said. He didn't care. They drove on what seemed quite a long way, and there was the sound of a lot more traffic. They won't find any blackberries here, he thought. Stupid twits. They were in a town, stopped on a main road. The woman got out. Jonathan prayed that he wouldn't have to move.

'Get out,' a voice said briskly. 'Let's have you! No messing about.'

He groaned.

'I told you,' the woman said indignantly. 'He's one of those—what do you call them?—I mean, he's stoned.'

'Junkies,' her husband said.

'On your feet,' the policeman said, scooping at Jonathan with his arm. Jonathan stumbled out. The policeman put a hand under his jaw, lifted his head up and peered into his face.

'What's your name?'

'Jonathan Meredith.'

The policeman's expression changed abruptly.

'Come again? Jonathan Meredith?'

'Yes.'

'The one we're looking for?'

'I daresay.'

'God Almighty,' the policeman said, grinning happily. His aggression melted into immediate affability. He turned to the woman and said, 'Where did you pick him up?'

'He was standing by the road, about five miles back. He asked for a lift. We didn't like the look of him, so we brought him here. We don't approve of this sort of thing— I mean, on a Sunday, young kid in that condition. What are they coming to, I said to Joe? It's not right. You say you're looking for him?'

'He's the most wanted person in the country at the moment, madam.'

The woman's eyes went round as saucers. The old bag, Jonathan thought, dumping me on the fuzz to get me into trouble! It's where he wanted to be, but she hadn't known that. He ignored her as she followed them up the steps. Thanks to her he was going to get home more quickly than he had bargained for, which thought did nothing to cheer him.

His arrival in the police station caused a great excitement. He had hoped for a cup of tea and an armchair, but after a quick session of telephoning the man who issued the orders had him out into a police car and on his way at some eighty miles an hour, blue light flashing and siren wailing. Lesser motorists pulled into the kerb as they sped past, goggling at their haste. Jonathan stared back, not convinced that it mattered as much as appearance suggested.

'Where've you been?' the policemen in the car asked. 'Where did they hide you up?'

'On a boat.'

'Where?'

'Sailing. It sailed to Holland and back.'

'Jeez!' they whistled, and the driver added another ten miles an hour to his speed.

'No wonder we couldn't find you! The only clue we turned up all the way was a bloody horse. Your friend NcNair—he brought it in—'

'A *horse*?' Jonathan didn't see at all.

'Traced to a Mrs Allsop. Stolen. No lead at all really. And then you walked in—'

'Where are we going? Home?'

'No. To old Marshall, to answer questions. You won't be through for hours yet.'

I should be so lucky, Jonathan thought! But he didn't want to go home either. He dreaded facing his parents. He hadn't known when he was well off, lying under those trees in the sunshine . . .

'Yes, I know, Arthur. The horse *is* Mrs Allsop's, but that doesn't get us any farther. I'm ringing to say he's turned up. Yes, that's what I said. Appeared in some police station or other out of the blue. He's with Inspector Marshall now. No, I haven't seen him yet. Yes, it's fantastic. I know. I feel a hundred years younger. Yes, they say he's all right. Suffering from the after effects of some drug or other—the doctor examined him. Apparently he's been on a boat, a yacht—yes, it's extraordinary. I don't know much yet. He has to answer all these questions, you see, in case they can catch up with the wretches. No, not terribly likely, I gather. It's wonderful to have him back, but it does make one so dreadfully angry—you know what I mean . . . yes . . . absolutely *infuriating*. One is so helpless. One feels so bitter . . . No, he's not hurt at all, just a bit dazed apparently. Somebody said he'd been taken to Holland and back—yes, sailing . . . well, yes, I always think he prefers sailing to riding, so perhaps he even enjoyed it, I don't know. I shall find out later on. Yes, Arthur, I knew you'd be glad to hear the news. Tell Peter—yes, he was really splendid. Goodbye, dear.'

'What did the old battle-axe say?'

'She doesn't know very much yet. He's with the police still. He's all right, but dazed, she said.'

'I hope she lays off him,' Peter said, remembering Jessica.

Mr McNair looked surprised. 'What an odd thing to say. What do you mean? I would have thought she'd be overjoyed to see him, not angry.'

Peter shrugged. 'You know her. She will at first, but later on, if they don't get the money back—'

'Don't be daft. It wasn't Jonathan's fault, surely?'

Peter grimaced, wishing he hadn't opened his big mouth. There were things the generations didn't agree on, and the motives of parents were one of them. Jessica, he guessed, had been unerringly accurate in her assessment of the situation.

'I'll go out and start feeding. Does the skinny mare get anything special?' When in doubt, change the subject.

———

Jonathan got out of bed very slowly. He had lain there as long as possible but it was now something to eleven, and he really couldn't put off getting up any longer. His mother had looked in twice already, but he had feigned heavy, recuperative sleep.

In fact he now felt perfectly well, apart from the fact that the room was still going up and down slightly, beating to windward in a force five. Outside it was fine, a glittering autumnal sun bright on the close-shaved lawns, a green woodpecker making holes in the perfection,

79

flashing like a jewel. Jonathan stood at the window watching. It was nicer than usual, after what had happened. Ordinarily it would have bored him, but now he preferred to stand looking at it than think back on what had happened. For some reason, he didn't want to think back on that at all. It was Monday, he remembered, and he should be back at school. He didn't want to go back to school either, or think about it. Looking at the lawns and the woodpecker was really nice.

After a bit he heard creaking on the stairs again, so crossed silently over to his own bathroom, locked the door and turned on the shower.

'Jonathan?'

He didn't answer. His lips still tasted salty and his hair was all salty too, not lathering for ages. But it didn't matter, he wasn't in a hurry. He stood there, the hot water running soothingly over his body and thinking, this is really nice. The simple things of life. Except that perhaps everybody didn't have their own bathroom suite. Jeez, perhaps they wouldn't either when the loss of the half million began to bite! Another thing he would rather not think about, the warm physical glow changing to a sick feeling of guilt. He kept feeling guilty, and yet no one had accused him of anything at all. No one had criticized. He sheered his mind away, back to physical things, and got dried and tried to discourage the tight corkscrew curls his hair always sprang into when wet, but without success. He got clean jeans and a faded red, much-darned jersey he was fond of, and dressed slowly, and eventually, after a long contemplation of his complexion in the mirror—which convinced him he could put off shaving for a good while yet—and a critical appraisal of his features—not bad really, he'd seen a lot worse—he opened the door and started downstairs.

The sun poured in through the thick smoky old glass

of the low windows in the hall, making slashes of gold across the floor. Jonathan caressed his favourite cherub of the little group carved into the newel post at the bottom of the staircase, and paused, and thought, yes, it was nice, what he took for granted, the pure pleasure of beautiful surroundings. He had never given it a thought before. But only rich children got kidnapped; nobody was held to ransom for fifty quid. It was only because of all this that it had happened.

There was a smell of bacon and coffee, which encouraged him. He walked down the flagged passage to the kitchen and went in. His mother was standing at the cooker, dressed in riding clothes, cooking the bacon.

'Hullo,' she said. 'I heard you getting up. Are you hungry now?'

He hadn't been last night, not hungry nor talkative either. He had dropped into bed and flaked out at once. The police had kept him till gone seven.

'Yes, I am quite.'

'Feel okay?'

'Yes.'

She smiled. 'No reason why you shouldn't have gone back to school in that case! Tomorrow perhaps. Jess wanted to stay at home, not to miss any excitement.'

'What excitement?'

It looked singularly peaceful to Jonathan.

'Oh, people keep ringing up. Reporters and suchlike. The television want to interview you. It was in the news, you see, quite an excitement.'

'God, how awful.'

'Well, better you walking in like that than a body turning up somewhere. I'm not complaining.'

'No, I suppose not. But I don't particularly want to be interviewed.'

'They might pay you.'

81

'You mean we need the money?' His voice sounded edgy, even to himself, and the guilt feeling came again. His mother looked at him a trifle sharply. Jonathan noticed that she looked thin in the face and had shadows under her eyes.

'I thought you might like it,' she said, mildly enough. 'Shall I fry some tomatoes?'

'Yes please.'

'The police rang up this morning. They know who did it, but they don't know where they are, except probably in Europe somewhere by now.'

'Yes, it wouldn't have been hard to trace them. Not with their being in that race, and *Jago* nearly colliding with them off Breskens. I told the police that *Jago* would know which yacht it was.'

'She was called *Orbit*. Belonged to a man whose son worked in your father's office until three months ago. Impeccable references: Winchester, Oxford, first-class degree—but in too much of a hurry to make money. The father is absolutely horrified—genuinely. '

'Well, it struck me—whoever planned it—they were clever. In everything, in every detail.'

'Yes. We paid up like lambs.'

Jonathan felt like a spider being stepped on. He shrugged, said nothing, poured himself a cup of coffee.

'Why on earth didn't you use the hairdryer?' his mother said. 'I'll have a cup of coffee too, while you're about it.'

Jonathan fetched another mug.

'I've been out on Florestan. Got to start getting him fit,' she said. 'I could eat a bit of bacon too, now I come to think of it.'

'Has Dad gone up to London?'

'Yes. Gone to sort things out a bit. It's all going to be rather difficult.'

Jonathan poured out the coffee. 'How . . . difficult?'

'Well, most people losing half a million pounds would consider the situation . . . difficult, to put it mildly.'

'You might get it back.'

'Unlikely, I understand. The snag was the lapse of time between them getting home in the yacht, and you being in a position to say what had happened. They got in at nine a.m., apparently, and you told the police what had happened round about two thirty. By that time, nearly six hours, they had collected the money and left the country.'

'Hmm.'

'What I can't understand—I don't know the full story yet; you'll have to enlighten me—is how they hid you at the end. They must have had the customs men aboard. They went aboard every yacht. And no one suspected a thing. That was the time . . . if you could have raised the alarm then—well, they would have been caught red-handed.'

Yes, well, that's where I failed, Jonathan thought, not wanting to think about it. That's what's on my conscience. But I'm not saying anything. His mother put a large plate of bacon, eggs, tomatoes, and fried bread down in front of him. It looked marvellous. He might feel a lot better afterwards. He started to eat.

'Where did they hide you?'

'In the life-raft case.'

After being so restrained about the idea of being tossed overboard, when the message had come through to say the money had been delivered, he hadn't been able to face the change of plan with the same restraint at all. He had not foreseen the alternative, standing there at the tiller gazing into the darkness. He had not realized that he would have to go through the life-raft horror again. Not until, with the coming of dawn, and the crew jubilant, he had been blindfolded again and taken below.

'You'll be okay, boyo—not to worry! We'll take you ashore and lock you up in a safe place while we make our disappearance, and then you'll be freed and home to the bosom of your family.'

That was when he had failed. The claustrophobic hell of the life-raft case was not to be contemplated sanely, and he hadn't managed a stiff upper lip any longer. It was an hour of his life which he would remember with shame until his dying day. He had asked to be dosed with the same tablets that he had fought so strenuously to reject some several hours previously and they, with amused contempt, had administered them along with a cup of tea. He had then remembered no more until his recovery in the wood. Even now, the very thought of being crammed down under the lid of that case had the power to bring him out in a sweat.

'I thought you said you were hungry?' his mother was saying, looking at him curiously.

He felt very sick, suddenly and unnervingly, and couldn't say anything. The feeling of self-contempt was pulverizing. He had refused to face the despicable, crawling cowardice of his behaviour until now, having pretended to the police that the drugs had been forced on him and avoided thinking about the issue ever since. But now, brought face to face with it by his mother, he knew he could never, never admit it—not to anyone, his caving in, his tears, his pleading, his craving to devour the oblivion pills. No wonder the memory of it put him off his breakfast! It wasn't a recollection to savour.

'Oh dear.' His mother, glancing at his colour, tactfully took the plate away. 'Would you feel better in the garden for a few minutes? It's a gorgeous morning.'

He got up and went outside and wandered unseeingly across the lawn, hunched against accepting any comfort from the joys of nature. Then, the nausea receding, he went back, knowing at least that he couldn't run away every time. He didn't have to admit, but he had to behave rationally. He wasn't so much of a coward that he couldn't do that.

'It's those drugs still reacting, I suppose,' his mother said.

It certainly was, Jonathan thought.

'It's okay,' he said. 'I'm sorry about the breakfast.'

'The dogs will eat it, don't worry. I suppose an experience like that takes some getting over. For us all, I might add.'

'Yes.' He sat down. He could face the coffee all right. He gazed at it. His mother, watching him, said, 'Is there anything about all this that—that you perhaps haven't said . . . that's upset you? More than the quite obvious things, I mean. I thought last night you seemed—I don't know—'

Jonathan kept his eyes on the coffee. 'No. Only the quite obvious things. It wasn't very nice.'

'No.' His mother lit a cigarette and inhaled heavily. She was silent for a few moments, then she said, 'Now you're back safe and sound, and it's all over, I can't tell you how bitter I feel about it. Against them, I mean. I understand now what people mean who have been robbed, about feeling physically assaulted. It's the *insolence* of it, the utter nerve. I have never felt so angry before, about anything. I had hoped so much, even after the money had been handed over, that they might have been caught. I shan't be happy until they are.'

Jonathan, into the ensuing silence, said nothing. He could sense his mother considering him, judging him, frustrated by not knowing exactly what had happened but not wanting to push him, irritated but not letting it show. The usual thing, exacerbated by events . . . they reacted one on the other, pushing each other into their worst attitudes: he, by retracting, clamming up, making her probe more than she knew was sensible, could see at the same time how and why it angered her. He too would be angry in her place. But he wanted to be left alone, to work out his own salvation, not to be told. The more he was told, the more he withdrew. With his father it was different; his father wasn't nearly so demanding and didn't care so much, and laughed a lot more, but his father wasn't there very often. His mother was always there. His father took his children as they came, but his mother wanted them her way.

'Well,' he said, relenting a fraction, 'they will probably be caught in the end.'

'They might be, I suppose.' She flicked the ash of her cigarette sharply into the ashtray, frowning. 'When they got back into Mersea, Sunday morning, there must have been so many people around—and there were police all over the place . . . there was a road-block on the Colchester road, I understand . . . I can see that you hadn't a chance to do anything while you were at sea, but if only then— when they were at such risk—'

'I was unconscious.'

'They drugged you?'

It was uncanny, as if she sensed, as if she *knew*—to put her finger on his vital failing, out of the whole bloody trip. Not to say how stupid he was taking the lift in the first place, or why didn't he jump ship at Breskens—but to home on to his raw nerve with her instinct for finding him out . . . it was completely in character, a part of their eternal relationship.

'Yes,' he said stubbornly. 'Before we got into Mersea. I didn't know a thing.'

'What did they use?'

'I don't know what it was. Pills.'

He could see her working out how feasible it was, to

force someone to take pills against their will. Or was he just thinking she was thinking that, because of his bad conscience?

'It must have been very unpleasant for you, the whole thing.'

'Yes.'

The telephone rang and she went out to answer it. Jonathan reached out for the cigarette she had laid in the ashtray and took some soothing inhalations, feeling angry with himself—for what he'd done and for her looking at him like that, and for the slimy sweat of self-contempt that kept coming like a physical sickness.

She came back quite soon and said, 'That was the BBC. They're sending someone to interview you for a news programme tonight.'

'You mean on television?'

'Yes. I said to come here. The police said you weren't to leave home in case they wanted you for anything.'

'I don't want to be on television.'

His mother looked amazed. 'Why ever not?'

Jonathan was appalled, and couldn't begin to describe what the thought of such total exposure did to his inner sanctum. Perhaps his expression showed it, for his mother said to him, quite patiently, 'Jonathan, it's time you grew up. It's a perfectly normal thing today, to be interviewed, if anything like this happens. People are interested. You've got to learn to face things like this.'

'Why?'

'It's a necessary thing in life, to be able to face the world with composure, and answer questions articulately.'

Jonathan found no words to express his outrage, both at being forced into a situation that was like a thousand dentist's appointments rolled into one, and at his mother's machine-like response, sane and commendable and utterly irrelevant.

'I—I—' He could feel himself changing colour, drained by his mother's logic.

'Take a grip of yourself, Jonathan. You're not a baby any more. It's not *Mastermind*. Only informal chat.'

Jonathan, steam-rollered, got up and left the room. He went to the telephone and rang the McNair's. While the bell was ringing he remembered that it was a normal school-day for everyone else, but before he thought to put the receiver down again, a voice answered with the number. It was Peter.

'It's Jonathan.'

'Hi. Nice to have you back. That'll teach you to go off with strange men.'

'You can say that again. What are you doing? I need to talk to somebody sane.'

'You've got the wrong number.'

'Could be. Are you otherwise engaged? Why aren't you at school?'

'I'm lame. Haven't they told you? You're not the only one who's been suffering, you know.'

'Can't you come over?'

'No.'

'Cripes, Peter, I want sanctuary. I'll be round.'

Jonathan could hear Peter thinking of something tactful to say and failing. He put down the receiver and went back into the kitchen to face his mother with composure and make an articulate announcement.

'I'm going to Peter's, if anyone wants me. And I'll be back before the box people get here. I'm not running away or anything.'

'I'm glad to hear it,' his mother said calmly. 'Don't wander though. You've got instructions to keep in touch. Back for lunch.'

'Okay.'

'You can go back to school tomorrow, I should imagine.'

Big deal, thought Jonathan gloomily.

He went out to get his bike and found it missing, remembered that it was a casualty of the abduction and took Jessica's. It took twenty minutes to Peter's, where he was received with a great continental embrace from Peter's stepmother, a hearty handshake from his father and a sardonic smile from Peter.

'How does it feel to be a million-dollar man, proved and paid up?'

'A bit burdensome. I'm not really sure that they wouldn't prefer the money.'

'Now, Jonathan—if you'd seen them, especially your mother,' Mr McNair said earnestly. 'I never thought I'd see the day when your mother—well, she was in a state. She cried.'

'She cried when Major was put down.'

'Well, there you are,' Peter said. 'Those mugs should've pinched Florestan. They'd have got their money just the same.'

Jonathan grinned, feeling better, but Mr McNair snapped at Peter, 'That's not really amusing. It's not at all funny—what happened.'

When they were on their own Peter said to Jonathan, 'His trouble is he's got no sense of humour. It did have its funny side, you know. At this end. Not at yours, I daresay.'

'No.'

'What happened then? I knew it was something to do with a boat, all along. I just knew. But I never said anything. I thought they'd be better at it than me. But they didn't turn anything up at all. I mean, it was me that brought the horse in—the only clue all along.'

'Horse?'

Peter explained about the horse, and what had happened at his end, and Jonathan told his side of the tale, leaving out the bit he wasn't going to tell anybody, not even Peter.

'Well, I don't see that you could have done anything,' Peter decided.

'Who is suggesting I could have?' Jonathan asked bitterly.

'Lawks, nobody,' Peter said, quickly remembering what Jessica had said, and wishing he wasn't so adept at putting his foot in it.

'That's what you think,' Jonathan said darkly.

'Explain yourself, boy. They've proved they love you half a million pounds' worth. What more do you want?'

'That they don't keep reminding me of the fact, that's all. And the fact that the blokes got clean away, laughing their heads off—that's what's needling my mother. She doesn't like being done. It hurts even more than the money, I think—she wants them caught.'

'I should think it's quite likely they will be, don't you? Everybody knows who they are.'

'They're bright though. Bright enough to work out how to stay hidden, I should imagine. It must be easier than the part they've already done, and they didn't make many mistakes there.'

'No, well, it'll all blow over eventually. Bound to. Even your mother can't go on grinding her gnashers for revenge for ever. Just keep out of her way—easy for you, once you're back at school.'

'School'll be pretty ghastly—going back, I mean. If it was in all the newspapers—'

'Yes, it is. Have you seen this morning's? You at the police station looking like a junkie heading for a padded cell, and me on Sirius biting back tears of emotion at hearing my friend is safe . . . you'll be a hero back at

90

school. Even I am looking forward to basking in reflected glory.'

'Yes, well, you—you're such a big-headed beggar you'll enjoy it. Tell you what, if you come back with me you can go on the box instead of me. The television people are on their way down now. How about it?'

'Yes! Better than mouldering here. I might be discovered. I'll come on Sirius—I bet they'd like a reel or two of him. You can get him ready for me—good idea.'

Mr McNair said acidly, 'The idea of your being off school is so that you can lie down and rest your leg.'

Peter said, 'One of your mottoes is, ''Seize your opportunities.'' I've heard you. That's all I'm doing. The BBC isn't down here every day of the week. I want to enlarge my experience.'

'I'll enlarge one of your ears if you carry on in that tone of voice, my lad.'

Peter tactfully shut up and hobbled down to the stable-yard with Jonathan, who tacked up Sirius for him and gave him a bunk up. They went back to Ravenshall, not hurrying, weaving down the leaf-thick lanes, Sirius followed by the bicycle.

'You'll soon be too big for that pony,' Mrs Meredith said to Peter, laying another place for lunch.

'Well, he's only got to last another ten days, until the Horse of the Year Show. Then he'll be sold to someone littler. I've got to start on pointers, me daddy says.'

'Is your ankle going to be all right by Wembley then? You'll never find anyone else to jump the brute, if it isn't.'

'Oh, it'll have to be. We're not going to miss that, our last public performance.'

'And then you're going into racing? You haven't got another showjumper to bring on?'

'No. At the moment I'm scheduled to work on a nag

called Garnet, which my father reckons will win all the point-to-points we take it to when it's fit.'

'And you reckon, too?'

'If we live to see the day, possibly.'

'Are you going into racing? Seriously, I mean?'

'Yes, I think so. But I want to go away from home. To a decent place. Next year probably.'

'Does your father want you to go away?'

'No, of course not. Lose his free labour.'

Mrs Meredith put on her non-committal face and turned back to the grill, where her Welsh rarebits were sizzling. She said, 'I was hoping Jonathan might get interested in racing. Florestan's going really well now. He's learned what it's all about. And I'm getting too long in the tooth to move out of the Ladies' Race—I'm not one of these toughie girls who'll ride in the Open.'

Peter, having thought her a very toughie girl ever since he first knew her, was tactful enough not to say so. He exchanged a sympathetic glance with Jonathan who said crossly, 'How can I be expected to ride point-to-points *and* go to boarding school? If you let me leave and sign on at the local comprehensive I'll ride your horse for you, I've told you.'

'Jonathan, it's not necessary to change schools. Racing is on a Saturday. I'll keep the horse fit, you can race it when you're home.'

'Yes, but how can *I* be fit enough, not riding in the week, only for the race? It's no good having a fit horse when all *I* do all the week is sit on a radiator and read books.'

'Don't exaggerate, Jonathan. I'm quite sure you do a lot more than that, the fees we pay.'

'I thought boarding schools had lots of games, to keep your mind off sex.'

'Really, Peter, must you be so crude? You're quite right,

of course, they do have lots of games. Jonathan's as fit as a fiddle. It's just his argument, you understand, because he wants to change schools.'

'Well, can't he? The comprehensive is okay.'

'You're there so little, Peter, you're hardly in a position to judge.'

Point to her, Peter conceded. He grinned. It was just like home, this arguing. He carried on like this with his father. Jonathan rolled his eyes, and then adjusted to inscrutability as his mother turned round with the plates.

'It would be terribly cheap,' he remarked, to the table. 'Now we've lost so much money.'

His mother sent him a daggers look, but anything she might have been going to say was interrupted by the sound of vehicles in the stable-yard.

'The BBC has arrived,' Peter announced.

Jonathan, taking no notice, started on his food. He was fed up with implied criticisms and his role in life and wanted to crawl into a hole. Which was the last of the options open to him, judging by the smart people he could see unloading in the yard. They were all obviously having a nice day out, and Jonathan saw that what had happened to him made jobs for people like them, and he didn't like the idea. He resented it bitterly. His mother looked at him and said warningly, 'Jonathan, you're to co-operate, you understand.'

She went to the door and opened it and they all came in. Jonathan was forced to abandon his Welsh rarebit and get up and shake hands politely with the producer, the interviewer, the cameraman, the sound man, the lighting man, the make-up girl, and the secretary, conscious of the expertise in their eyes on his face, of their shrewd, arrogant appraisal of his surroundings, of their general bursting confidence and assumption of authority. His mother took them through into the sitting-room for drinks, as the producer kindly insisted on the boys finishing their lunch, and then came back to tell Jonathan to change.

'Change?' said Jonathan, looking blank.

'You can't appear in that dreadful jersey. Go and put something on without holes in—a shirt and tie.'

'But—' Jonathan made a great effort to keep calm. 'These are the clothes I wear,' he said gently. 'The holes are all darned. I like this jersey. I am going to wear it.'

'Jonathan—' Mrs Meredith's eyes were sending out sparks. Peter watched her, fascinated. Much to his disappointment she was called at this point by the producer to work out backgrounds, and the boys were left to finish the last glutinous globs of cheese on their plates.

'Cripes, I wish I was dead,' Jonathan said. 'I wish they'd chucked me overboard. She'd far rather have had the money. I wish they'd all electrocute themselves. I wish they were all dead too.'

'Steady on,' Peter said, grinning.

'I can't stand people like them.'

'Sour grapes. You want to be a smoothie too, but you don't know how.'

'Oh, jeez, I can't do this.'

'You're so bloody stupid, Meredith. You only have to jaw at that bloke in the mauve shirt. You don't have to act. And then they'll pay you and go away. It's peanuts. God, it'll make a change from all those po-faced trades union professional spouters and social worker ladies from outer Birmingham—a fine clean-limbed lad like you back from the jaws of death.'

'I didn't know where I was well off.'

'I think we'll have some outdoor shots,' somebody was saying loudly in the doorway. 'The light is fantastic on those lawns. Get him walking across towards the house, long shot, kicking the leaves perhaps, get all that lovely Elizabethan front—that red jersey, just the thing.

Look, if you're ready—Jonathan, is it?—perhaps you'd do this thing for us? Introduction, you see—you in your background, and then cut to close-up and Humphrey will ask you some questions about what happened. We're not going to rehearse that, if it's all right by you. Humphrey's technique works better with an unrehearsed interviewee. You've probably seen how he does it, you must know his work? No problem. Now, while we're setting the camera up outside, can we clear this table then, and Dolly can put her things here and do your make-up. Sorry to be so snappy about all this but you understand we're a news programme and we have to move fast. We've a dog to see in Harpenden before we go back, had eighteen puppies we're told, would you believe it? In here, Dolly, there's a love. And as soon as you're ready we'll have you on the lawn by the big beech tree. Okay?'

'Puke,' said Jonathan, as the man disappeared out of the kitchen door, trailed by several of the retinue.

'Which of you is it, then?' Dolly said, dumping her box on the table.

'It's him,' Peter said. 'A bit easier than those eighteen puppies in Harpenden, I should imagine. They'll be a bit tricky.'

'Come again?' Dolly chewed gum and worked deftly with hypnotic, green-nailed fingers. Jonathan, looking much sharper round the edges, trailed outside and dutifully kicked leaves all the way across the lawn to the front door. He stopped, hands in pockets, and looked enquiringly towards the producer.

'Fine. We'll have the actual interview inside, in the hall. Humphrey fancies the Tudor chimney-piece.'

The hall was lit strongly by imported lamps on long arms. Jonathan waited around while the camera arrived through the door and was set in place, feeling progressively worse, the Welsh rarebit lying uneasily. He could see his mother eyeing him critically, working out what sort of an impact her son was likely to have on the viewing horde. Dolly was advancing with a comb. Jonathan scowled heavily, stood where he was pushed, relaxed to order, smiled, scowled again and tried to pretend that Humphrey was just any man asking idiot questions about his experiences. Unfortunately Humphrey seemed more interested in what Jonathan's feelings had been than what had actually happened and Jonathan was not going to talk about his feelings.

'Were you really afraid at any time that you weren't going to come out of it alive?'

'Yes, at one time.'

'Did they tell you they were going to throw you overboard?'

'No, they didn't tell me, but I heard them discussing it when they thought I was asleep.'

'And how did you feel about that?'

Jonathan found himself looking towards his mother, who had expected him to be articulate. 'Well . . .' He felt a great urge to say, 'How would you have felt, you ape-faced berk?' He shrugged.

'How did you feel when they told you the money had been delivered?'

'I—' The words didn't exist for the great tangle of emotion that had enmeshed him. Didn't the sweating, smiling Humphrey have even a thimbleful of imagination—to see that one just couldn't, leaning against one's home hearth, recapitulate in a pithy sentence the mental turmoil of that strange night.

'I can't explain. It all seems very unreal now.' A good articulate sentence, with correct grammar, firmly enunciated. He gazed expectantly at Humphrey.

'I'm sure it does. It does seem to be a story of extraordinarily clever planning on the part of these kidnappers. And what intrigues me is the ingenuity of the way they took you ashore under the noses of all those people going about their Sunday morning business, even, I believe, past a police block. Perhaps we can show the viewers how they managed this? I managed to get hold of a life-raft, similar to the one used by the kidnappers in this case. Here it is.'

Somebody appeared at Jonathan's side, dragging a life-raft case which was opened on the hearth-rug. Humphrey bent over it, smiling up into the camera.

'Just large enough for a body—and the weight of the body very similar to the weight of the raft when inside. The case cannot be opened without the life-raft going into action—that is, inflating itself ready for action, so when the police searched the van they didn't open the case. I believe I'm right in saying that once the life-raft is inflated the whole works has to go back to the manufacturer at considerable cost to be repacked for use again, so naturally the police, having no reason to suspect this party, didn't pursue their search to those lengths. Now, Jonathan, if they had—'

Humphrey straightened up, still smiling relentlessly. 'If they had, perhaps you would show us what they would have found? Would you show us how very neatly a person of your size can be hidden, fitted into this case?'

Jonathan looked at Humphrey in astonishment.

'No.'

Humphrey looked slightly pop-eyed. 'Just get in it, I mean, the way you did—'

'I never got in it. I was *forced* into it—' The camera had come very close, and the lights seemed to Jonathan to flare up like hot suns, burning him up. He felt the sweat breaking out. He looked at the life-raft case and felt the panic rising, the air draining away out of his lungs, the awful burning feeling flooding out of the very pit of his being. Humphrey seemed suddenly very far away, and still disappearing.

'No, I won't—'

How very strange, Jonathan thought. Humphrey had gone. He fell in a flat faint on the hearth, and the producer said, 'Cut, for God's sake.'

When he came round he was lying on the sofa in the sitting-room with his mother sitting beside him looking thoughtful. Through the door into the hall he could see the lights and the camera, and Peter chatting to Humphrey, who was finding it hard to get a word in edgeways. Jonathan didn't say anything, remembering without any difficulty what had happened. Seeing his mother's face he knew he could sink no lower in her regard, but it really didn't seem to matter. There was absolutely nothing to say.

To his surprise, his mother kissed him kindly and said, 'Never mind, old chap. Let's forget it now. It hasn't been very nice for you.'

9

Jonathan duly returned to school and was forced to suffer his new role of national celebrity, which fortunately did not last long. In the familiar, circumscribed confines of his monastic boarding school it was tedious but not unbearable. He learned to tell the tale as articulately as his mother would have wished, not flinching at parts he would rather have forgotten, but lying fluently to cover them up. He had to very carefully blank out a part of his mind when he described his confinement in the life-raft case, because if he once allowed his memory full rein to dwell on how it had affected him he began to get the same symptoms: the feeling of suffocation and the panic that came with it started to make his voice shake. The first time it happened was with his interview with his headmaster on his return, and he was so terrified of going out of control and repeating the humiliating Humphrey episode that he stopped quite deliberately and switched his mind to something else. It took a great effort and the effect was slightly strange. There was a waste-paper basket beside the head's desk, where he was sitting, and a letter was lying on top which said, 'Dear Mr Armstrong, In view of the fact that my son Antony (Lower V B) by reason of his abnormally fast growth this last year now has to wear size 12 shoes, I would be obliged if . . .' The rest was hidden by a scatter of discarded cigarette ends out of the ashtray, but the distraction was sufficient to steady the threatened dreadful disintegration. The feeling of panic, faced by the vision of Antony's enormous feet, receded. Jonathan, by concentrating very hard, was able to get back on course, moving delicately over the deep abyss without actually looking in. It was an enormous achievement, and the relief that came with it was beautiful. The headmaster was looking at him rather strangely.

'Are you all right?' he asked.

'Yes, perfectly all right.' Pausing to read the discarded correspondence had seemed a little eccentric, but so much more tactful than throwing a hysterical faint on the head's carpet. Jonathan was so grateful for the power he had raised to exorcise the threatened humiliation that he continued his story with almost euphoric carelessness. The next time he told it, to his room-mate Ashworth, he experimented with the same trick, switching his mind when he came to the shaky part—this time to a yellow-hammer that happened to be sitting on the windowsill and trying to remember its Latin name—and, although the hiatus caused Ashworth to prompt him with, 'Then what?', it saved him from getting overtaken by the horrors. Once more the feeling of relief was overwhelming.

'Holy Cow, I wish something exciting would happen to me,' Ashworth said, lying on his back on his bed with the pillow over his head. 'Some people have all the luck. I couldn't believe it when I saw your mug in the papers, and read how much they wanted for you. Fabulous! It must have made you feel really great.'

Jonathan didn't follow the reasoning, a common lack on his part when talking to Ashworth. 'Yeah, it's really great to be kept tied up and blindfolded and starved and drugged for three days.'

'Yes, but when you came back—all that excitement and everyone being so pleased to see you and going on the box and the news and everything. I think that's really great.'

Jonathan sighed heavily, wondering how a mentality like Ashworth's had managed to acquire nine O-levels. Peter had a theory that if you had a lot of O-levels it didn't necessarily mean you were intelligent, only that you were good at learning. Peter said it wasn't the same thing at all. Ashworth seemed to bear him out. Peter was far more intelligent than Ashworth but had only got three. However, as Peter only attended school spasmodically, just enough to keep his father out of court, it was hard to evaluate.

Not long after returning to school Jonathan got a letter from home to say that his parents were going to Switzerland and he wouldn't be able to go home at weekends. Jessica also sent him a letter slightly more communicative than the one from his parents: 'Daddy has got to go on business but I think Mummy is going because your kidnappers are supposed to be in Switzerland and she thinks she might track them down! She really is a bit neurotic about it, I think, wanting them to be caught so badly. It's not as if catching them will get the money back. They are talking about selling some of the paintings but I think with taxes it is rather complicated and the government takes most of the money. They do go on about it, it is terribly boring, you can't imagine. I shall be glad to stay at school and you will too if you have any sense. Mummy seems to think it's all your fault and keeps saying, if only Jonathan had managed to do this or that, whatever she happens to think of, and Daddy tells her not to be daft and they have another row. I suppose it will all die down eventually . . .' Not, Jonathan thought, the most tactful of letters, especially to a conscience as jumpy as his. Mummy wasn't as far out as the rest of the family thought she was. If he hadn't been drugged at the end he might well have . . . well, he might have managed . . . what? No answer. But he wouldn't have the dragging-down feeling that Jessica's letter provoked, where in fact he agreed with his mother.

He lay in bed that night, listening to the grampus breathing of the portly Ashworth in the other bed, depressed and aimless in spirit. Unlike his mother, he had a sneaking regard for the prowess of the chief kidnapper, a whizz-kid of obviously ruthless ambition called Peregrine Corder. He had pulled a clever job, in Jonathan's opinion, and had shown a cool and considerable nerve that Jonathan envied. It had occurred to Jonathan several times that if Corder had thrown him overboard after he had heard that the money had been delivered, he would in fact have got away with his crime without anyone knowing who he was. But due to a certain dubious sense of honour, not to add mercy—and spurred, no doubt, by elation at the success of his plan—he had acknowledged the deal by delivering his hostage to safety, confident, presumably, that he could remain out of the hands of the law in spite of the information that Jonathan would pass on. Jonathan admired this confidence. His father had said, pityingly, 'Silly young idiot—with his brains he could have made half a million legitimately, given ten years or so—why the hurry?' But Jonathan thought Corder was an adventurer at heart and had enjoyed planning his coup. Even to the cunning theft of Mrs Allsop's hunter for collecting the money (it had been out at grass and not even missed): it was all admirably inventive and in fact, given the attitude of mind, positively enjoyable for them, with enough risk to set the adrenalin running, but very little tediousness involved. It was probably this element of cockiness that so enflamed his mother.

With the whole incident very much on his mind he fell asleep. Several hours later Ashworth dreamed that somebody was beating on the bedroom door, screaming for admittance, and woke up very abruptly. Somebody was indeed screaming: Ashworth, not an imaginative boy, scrambled out of his blankets to grope for the light-switch, blundering in his fright, and discovered that it was Jonathan who was screaming, lying on his bed with all the covers kicked off, white as the pillow itself.

'Meredith, you idiot! What's up?'

Ashworth had no experience of the tricks of the subconscious and it took him several seconds to comprehend that Jonathan was still asleep, although he was shouting, 'No! No! No!' and flailing about with his arms and legs with stupendous energy so that his bed was thumping the wall.

'Hey, *idiot*—' Ashworth went as close as he dared and hissed, 'Wake up, you fool! Jonathan!' Then, not wanting to get thumped, he went to the wash-basin, filled a glass with cold water and threw it in Jonathan's face. Behind him the door opened and Parsons, the head prefect, put his head round, saying 'What the hell's going on here?' Footsteps sounded down the corridor and lights were being switched on. Ashworth, slightly breathless in his agitation, stood looking down at the silenced, gasping, blue-lipped face hanging over the side of the bed and wondered if he'd done the wrong thing. He knelt down and grasped Jonathan by the shoulders and started to shake him.

'Meredith! Are you all right? For God's sake—'

'Leave him alone!' Parsons said. 'That's not the way.' He kicked Ashworth out of the way. 'Are you awake, Meredith? It's okay now. You're only dreaming.'

'What's happened?' Fletcher, the housemaster, tousled and shaggy in a vast camel-haired dressing-gown, yawned his way round the door.

'It's Meredith, dreaming—'

'God almighty, what about?'

'I don't know.' Parsons, looking at Jonathan, thought it must have been more terrible than anything in his own limited experience. He had never seen an expression like it. He was moved to reassure him again, in a voice far gentler than most people would have recognized as the head prefect's, 'It's okay now. It wasn't *real*.'

Jonathan rolled over away from him and buried his face in the pillow. 'It was real,' he said.

He wouldn't say anything else, not even when they fetched matron and he was fed hot sweet tea and regaled with reassurances and hearty common-sense advice and tucked up with extra blankets for his shivering.

'It would help to discuss it, Jonathan,' matron said briskly, 'to tell us what it was. All these things are better brought out in the open, you know. It's only by talking about these things freely that you can be helped.'

Jonathan didn't agree, and said so. They left him with a bedside light and hot-water bottle, listening to the footsteps receding, light-switches going off, the disturbed muttering in the bedrooms all down the corridor, all discussing Meredith's neurosis, and Ashworth's pig-like grunts as he rolled about to find the position that most encouraged his deep, uninhibited sleep. Jonathan would not risk going to sleep again, steeped in the knowledge that he was an even worse failure than he had supposed, not only incapable of foiling a mere kidnapper or two, but weak enough to allow the knowledge of his failure to unhinge him completely. He was thrown by this betrayal in unconsciousness, for it was not a weakness easily combatted. Impossible, in fact, to control the brain when asleep. And the actual nightmare, the feel of it, was better not recalled at all, for it had been horrific, the real event magnified to an unbearable degree by all the super-sensitive machinery of the subconscious, blown up by guilt and self-disgust. Jonathan was not so dim that he didn't understand all the reasons for what had happened. He didn't need matron's hearty theories paraded in order to understand what it was all about. Nobody was going to find out what was disturbing him, even if he screamed the place down every night.

Which he didn't—quite.

'Only every other night,' as a weary Ashworth put it.

'Meredith will have to be sent home,' the matron told the headmaster.

'He can't go home. His parents are abroad.'

'They must be told. He needs professional help. It's very bad for everyone, and the boy will be really ill if he goes on like this.'

'I'm assuming it's something to do with his being kidnapped? He never had nightmares before.'

'I assume so too, but he won't tell us what it's all about. We know it's the same thing every time—but that's all we know. It's obviously something quite terrifying, you can tell by his face and his behaviour, and when he comes to, his expression is—oh, it's quite indescribable. It's just not something we can cope with at all, I'm afraid. Nothing like the ordinary nightmare—we've had plenty of those, no trouble at all—something they've eaten, or the odd upset. This is quite different.'

'I'll get in touch with his parents. We have an address, of course.'

'I'll tell him then?'

'Send him to me. I'll see if I can find anything out.'

He did.

'Going home won't make any difference,' Jonathan said. 'I'd rather stay here really.'

'But you're not getting any sleep. Look at you—you've lost weight and you look ill. Your marks aren't good. You have to regard this as a form of sickness, you know. You must be treated for it properly, and it isn't the school's province to arrange this.'

'Look, I know perfectly well what's causing it, I don't need a psychiatrist to tell me.'

'Meredith, kindly take the advice of your elders and betters for a change. You know what's causing it—so much the better. But you can't stop it happening, can you?'

'No.'

'You want to, I take it? If you refuse help, I understand that to mean that you are quite content to go on suffering these nightmares. Is that true?'

'No.'

'Well then, stop being stubborn about it. Either you go home and your mother must deal with it, or, if you stay here, I will call in Dr Jenkins and you will have to co-operate in getting yourself straightened out. As from now you are off lessons, and in the sick bay.'

Jonathan was cornered. He stood in front of the head's desk fidgeting with the knob of a mechanical calendar, staring into space.

'Leave that alone,' the head said, 'and give me an answer.'

'It will cure itself in a little while, I'm sure. I'm not going to—to talk to anybody about it.'

'You go home then. I shall ring your parents in Switzerland immediately.'

'It will be worse with my mother around.'

'You will accept no help here. You give me no alternative, Meredith. The rest of us want to get some sleep too, you know.'

'Yes, I'm sorry.'

'*I'm* sorry too. For an intelligent boy you are being extremely difficult to help. Now sit down, and I will see if I can contact your mother. We have a telephone number in Zurich . . .'

He called in his secretary to put the call through, and started on some paperwork at his desk while he was waiting. Jonathan sat gazing at the carpet, thinking how furious his mother was going to be. She wouldn't understand, not in a million years, what it was all about. All she was bothered with was the fact that she had been swindled out of a lot of money by some young upstart who was a lot cleverer than she was, and until she got even with him she was not going to forget it. A few nightmares . . . he could just imagine her trying to work out why that meant she had to come home. She would say, 'See that he doesn't eat any cheese for tea. It must be something he's eaten.' Or, 'Tell him to pull himself together.' She was always saying people ought to pull themselves together. And what if he went home, and she came home to look after him? The idea was unbearable, the two of them together in the house with nothing to do but wait for him to have a nightmare. Jonathan looked at the headmaster desperately, and said, 'Must you call my mother?'

The headmaster, concentrating on something else, looked up and said, 'I beg your pardon?'

'I don't want to go home.'

The headmaster put his pen down and said, very evenly, 'You will talk to Dr Jenkins about it then? And see a specialist if he advises it? Today? Co-operate, Meredith?'

If he hadn't said 'today', it might have been possible. Jonathan thought of a trained psychiatrist getting to work on all his inadequacies and traumas and his mother complex and his great guilt about . . . about breaking down . . . and the nightmare, talking about the nightmare . . . it just wasn't possible; it was inconceivable . . .

The headmaster said, gently, 'You do need the help, Meredith. Look at you, now. We don't want to bully you.

We want you back to your old cheerful self. You've gone through a very nasty experience, it's nothing to be ashamed of if you can't cope with your feelings just now.'

His tone of voice made Jonathan furious.

'It doesn't matter.' His voice shook. He daren't say anything else. At least, if he had to go home, it would take a day or two for his mother to make arrangements, it would give him a bit more time. He might, in fact, be able to pull himself together.

The phone rang. The head picked it up, listened to the message and said to Jonathan, 'The call has come through. Do you want me to go ahead with it?'

Jonathan nodded.

The head said, in a different tone of voice altogether, 'Mrs Meredith? Yes, it's Armstrong here, from Meddington. I'm sorry to trouble you . . . well, yes, we have a spot of bother. Nothing really serious, but we feel Jonathan should be at home for a little while. He's having some nervous trouble, nightmares and so on, and you must realize it's very difficult for us to cope with it. I wouldn't have got in touch with you if I didn't feel it was absolutely necessary.'

Long pause for reaction, some soothing. 'Quite so, I do agree . . .' And then, 'He really does need some professional help, and I can't take decisions of this nature without your . . . no . . . no . . . I knew you would understand. I do appreciate it, yes, but . . . Yes. Yes. Very well. We'll expect you. That's splendid. Goodbye, Mrs Meredith.'

He put down the receiver.

'She says she'll fly home this afternoon. Her car is at the airport and she'll pick you up this evening.'

'This evening?'

It was still today then. He was no better off at all for

his choice. He was so indignant, he opened his mouth to protest, but couldn't find the words he wanted. He sat there with his mouth open and felt the tears trickling up and running down his cheeks like a mountain stream. He was so ashamed he wanted to die.

10

I t started with Peregrine Corder, whose face, although Jonathan had never seen it, was now perfectly familiar to him in his dream, and always the same, saying to him, quite kindly, 'If you eat these pills you won't know anything about it. You will have a lovely sleep and wake up at home.' Jonathan then ate the pills, about fifty of them in the dream, and rather dry and difficult to get down. This was when the first feeling of uneasiness came. Then Peregrine said, 'Now you get in the life-raft case,' and Jonathan replied, 'But not until the pills have worked and I've gone to sleep,' and Peregrine said, 'I can't help it if they don't work. It was you who wanted the pills. You've got to get in the life-raft case.' The life-raft case was open on the floor, only it was in the hall at home, not on the boat. The sunlight was shining through the smoky glass making the inside of the case look greenish, and it came nearer and nearer, getting bigger and bigger, and something was pressing Jonathan on the back of the neck, very strongly, so that he was forced to get right up close to the case. He started to struggle. A man in a mauve shirt then appeared and said, 'Would you show us how very neatly a person of your size fits into this case?' and he replied, 'But the pills haven't worked and I am still awake.' 'It doesn't make any difference. You have to get in. We haven't time to hang around,' and a lot of people started forcing him into the case, pressing him down heavily and squeezing the lid down over his back so that he was crushed up into the smallest possible space, pressed on all sides and without any air to breathe. He tried to struggle but there was no space to move even a finger, just the dreadful, burning pressure all round him. He started to shout out and Peregrine's voice said, very quietly and evenly, 'It's no good. He'll have to go overboard. The pills haven't worked.' And the life-raft case started to sink into the deep water, quite slowly, so that the water came in through the lid in a slow trickle. The life-raft case went on sinking and the water came up gradually, cold now, when it was hot before, over his knees and slowly over his back. In the dream he could lift his head up now, but no higher than his horizontal back, because it was then up hard against the lid, and he could look down into the case, which was now quite light, and see the water rising up towards his face, no longer slowly, but quite fast. It seemed to have a long way to come, much further than just from his knees on the bottom, but it came very fast, and he could hear himself screaming, and feel his head pressed down so that he couldn't move away, but had to watch it. He screamed and screamed, and Peregrine said, 'I would have thought all those pills would have worked by now,' and the water touched his nose and his mouth, and he woke up.

He saw his mother's face by the bedside lamp, white as a sheet, terrified. She looked terrible. He couldn't say anything, exhausted. He could feel the sweat trickling down his face and his body and the pressure still on the back of his head, hard up against the headboard of the bed. He was lying sideways, the quilt in a heap on the floor. He was freezing cold and shaking all over. He wanted to say to his mother, because of her face, that it was all right now, but he couldn't speak. He had to wait for it all to go away; it was so dreadful. It took a little while. This was when, at school, matron appeared, and Parsons was very kind, and Ashworth stood there saying,

'Bloody hell, I can't stand it.' But this time there was just the two of them, and his clock ticking loudly on the bedside table.

'Oh, Jonathan, I see what they mean,' his mother said softly. 'What is it? What's it all about?'

He had never heard her sound so meek and helpless, never guessed she could. It shook him almost as much as the nightmare.

'Are you cold?'

Yes, of course, sea water in March was very cold. It took ages to stop shivering. He groped for the edge of the quilt, and she covered him up and put the pillows straight and said, 'I'll go and make you a cup of tea.'

When she came back they had both had time to recover, and when she asked, 'What's it all about then? What do you dream about?' Jonathan was able to reply quite calmly, 'Being shut in a life-raft case. It's always the same. Being squashed in and the lid shut down.' Full stop, he thought. That's all you're getting.

'I can guess the effect it had on you. It all goes back to that time when Biddy Parkinson shut you in the boot of the Austin—do you remember? You were about five at the time. You've been funny about small cramped spaces ever since. You wouldn't go through the cave entrance in that French gorge—do you remember that?'

Jonathan was amazed, and looked at her over the tea-cup. 'You mean, there's a reason?'

'Well, partly. It must have been a terribly tight fit, and if one already has a phobia about cramped spaces—well, your reaction seems to me not entirely unexpected.' She then shot him a very shrewd look, went on to say something else, and stopped herself.

Mildly, she said, 'Drink up then. You're all right now? It doesn't happen again—not twice in one night?'

'No.'

'We'll talk about it in the morning.'

Not excited by the thought, Jonathan drank up and slept dreamlessly until nine o'clock, when he got up and went downstairs. The house seemed strange, the animals all farmed out, the rooms tidy and uncreased. His mother had got some food out of the freezer and was cooking breakfast. This was how it was before, Jonathan thought, after Humphrey's visit; it will go on the same way. It's worse than being at school. There's absolutely nothing that can make it all come right. The thought of living at home with just his mother until he stopped having nightmares was unbearable.

'Cheer up, Jonathan. It's not as bad as all that. We can sort it out.' His mother put mugs and sugar and milk on the table, and turned back to the pan on the stove. 'Do you want tea or coffee?'

'Tea, please. I don't want to stay here—I'd rather be back at school. They made me—I didn't want them to ring you up.'

'I know. Old Armstrong told me, says you refused to see a doctor. I don't want to stay here either. I want to go back to Zurich to your father. So we'll have to work something out.'

'Yes.'

'Make the tea, and I'll tell you what I propose.'

She hadn't wasted any time, Jonathan realized: she never did. He hadn't been able to see a solution to the mess he was in for weeks, but she had worked it out in less than twenty-four hours.

'I had a chat with that headmaster of yours. He said he wanted you to see a psychiatrist and talk over what was troubling you, making you have nightmares. Well, I agree with you—I'd have refused too—I think it's a load of old rubbish, a boy of your age—I told him so. It's quite plain to me that you're upset about what happened. It was a very nasty experience and it doesn't surprise me that it's given you nightmares. But I'm not going to sit here and say, "There, there, darling"—don't think that. What happened to you was very unpleasant, but then what happened to us—all that money . . . you don't seem to understand, you children, you take it so much for granted—but that money was, to your father and me, part of a life's work. We didn't inherit it, or make it by luck. We made it by sheer hard work and brains. We had nothing, when we started. You are so used to all this now—' She swept her hand round in an expansive gesture to indicate the undoubtedly affluent surroundings—'You don't remember the days when it was so hard, when we had nothing, when we both worked our guts out to get the business started. Even now, your father never rests, never takes a holiday, never stops thinking about his work. It's not as if it was just half a million lying in the bank amongst a whole lot of millions that had fallen from heaven. It was working money that's all got to be earned again. That's why I feel so bitter against these young men, so vindictive. *We* had to earn it, every penny, so who are *they*, to take it from us by such an underhand trick? God, they aren't even poor themselves! They're idle, spoilt young opportunists now laughing their heads off in some plush resort. Every time I think of them my blood boils! That all our work, our striving, has gone to keep them in luxury somewhere! And every time we see the police they say, "We're working on it, Mrs Meredith. It takes time." And I want to scream and rage and spit—I've never been patient and understanding and forgiving—it's just not in my nature. You know it, I daresay, for better or for worse.'

'You can't help what you are,' Jonathan agreed. 'Any more than I can.'

'A very clever remark, Jonathan, I grant you. But you're

still young enough to be moulded, and while it's in my hands you will go the way I want you to. And the point of this exercise now, is not that we all sit round and comfort you. That's not my way, Jonathan. I've never spoilt you, and I'm not going to start now, because you're going through a bad patch. You've got to learn to stand on your own feet, work out your own salvation. I shall never be easy on you, Jonathan, you know that, you know the way I am. But one day you will be glad of it, if not now.'

Jonathan, having gathered all this over the years, without having had it explicitly explained, found it hard to take, but could form no reasonable argument against the philosophy. There was no answer to her. As she had said herself, for better or for worse . . . one was lumbered by God with one's parents, and had no redress.

'At the moment—to come to the point—there's only one course that seems to me practical,' she continued, as he made no comment. 'We don't want to sit looking at each other here, both of us, and they won't have you at school, so I'm proposing that you go out and get a job, and work so hard that you'll be too tired at night to do anything but sleep like a top. I thought with Arthur. You know the work—there's masses to do there; he's always short of hands.'

'You mean at McNair's?'

'Yes. He's got three point-to-point horses in training, besides Florestan who went over there when we went to Zurich, and the hunters he hires out, not to mention all the ones he's buying and selling all the time. If you work there and take charge of Florestan, you can ride him in all the races after Christmas. Good, physical work—just what you want—you spend too much of your time mulling things over. You want to get some more flesh on you and some colour in your cheeks. I'll ring Arthur as soon as we've finished breakfast.'

'You mean work as a groom at McNair's?' Jonathan said, wanting to get it quite right.

'Exactly.'

'And live there, or here?'

'You'd better come back here for a few days in case you have any more nightmares. We can't subject them to that sort of bother. But if, as I hope, the way of life cures you, you can live in their groom's quarters and make a proper job of it.'

Jonathan, amazed, started on his toast and marmalade, making no comment. He didn't really know what he felt about the idea. It seemed, health-wise, quite a good one, and there would be Peter, and he knew everyone, and he wouldn't mind living over there. He wasn't so sure about all the hard physical work, knowing that Arthur McNair was a renowned taskmaster, but he wasn't afraid of hard work. More afraid of finding it boring than anything. But it wasn't a bad alternative: he couldn't think of a better.

'How long for?'

'Oh, till you're quite over all this. Perhaps till next spring, if you want to ride Florestan in his races.'

She wanted him to do that. It suited her, he knew. But it wasn't anathema to him either.

'You're well ahead with your school work,' she said. 'Six months off won't hurt you. Shall I ring Arthur now, or is there anything you're doubtful about?'

'No. If he'll have me, I don't mind.'

The more he thought about it, the more it appealed. His work at school, where he was taking maths and English and law, was difficult and exacting, and flying about the countryside on a posse of race-horses sounded quite attractive by comparison.

To bring him down to earth, his mother said, 'Florestan does two hours trotting on the roads every morning, and I dare say the others do too. So, riding and leading, that's four hours work for somebody every day. Even if you were just to take that over, and nothing else, I reckon you'd sleep better at nights.'

She got up and went to the telephone and he heard ominous phrases floating back through the door . . . 'No, Arthur, not to swan around, but to work hard, really hard . . . well, he's got some hang-ups over this business, and the school has sent him home. It's a mental thing, and I think the cure lies in a complete change . . . yes, we'll talk it over when we come. Fine . . . Florestan? . . . yes, splendid, I'm looking forward to seeing him. In an hour's time then—goodbye, Arthur.'

She came back looking pleased and business-like.

'That's settled then.'

No wonder, Jonathan thought, she'd made a fortune by middle age. She was hard and overwhelming, like the North face of the Eiger.

'Go and get some suitable clothes—you'll want jodhpurs if you're going to exercise. They're in the middle drawer.'

Two hours later, somewhat bemused, Jonathan was riding a thoroughbred called Garnet and leading a dark brown hunter mare called Birdsong along a lane away from McNair's with instructions not to be back until twelve thirty and 'three-quarters of that time to be at the trot, please.' He had been given a route of some ten miles, all up and down hill. It was raining slightly, and cold, and he couldn't quite believe it, the mind numb, neither liking nor not liking, but recalling with amazement that only this time the day before he had been summoned to the headmaster's office and put on the sick list. Arthur McNair had taken one look at him and said to his mother, 'Good God, the boy looks like a scarecrow! Haven't they been feeding him or something?' 'It's not that, Arthur dear. He's not well, I told you. That's why he's here.' Some cure, Jonathan thought!

After lunch he was to do another ten miles with two more horses. 'If you've got the strength,' McNair had said doubtfully. At least he had been promised one of Mrs McNair's famous spaghettis for lunch, which might see him through. Having been off his feed for several weeks, the thought of it, after five miles, was encouraging. After ten miles he could think of nothing else.

'Well,' said McNair, 'that's put some colour in your cheeks at least. Can you do it again? Maggie can go if not. There's a three-year-old to be lunged, all the tack to be cleaned for hunting tomorrow, and any amount of grooming, if you prefer to stay at home.'

So much for the alternative. He went again, with Florestan and a black gelding who tried to tear his arm out of its socket every five minutes, and when he got back and had put the horses away and cleaned them up, he had their tack to do and a white mare out of the field to clean up for a prospective buyer. He had got most of the mud off and was washing her tail in a bucket of hot water and soap powder in the yard when Peter cycled in from school. His tuneless whistling died in astonishment when he recognized Jonathan.

'What on *earth*—?'

'Your father's new stable-hand,' Jonathan explained. The mare wouldn't stand still and Peter dropped his bike and went to her head out of sheer force of habit.

'I don't get it, Meredith. Explanation please. Stand still, you wall-eyed weed. Get her up against the wall and I'll make her stay.'

They got her cornered and Jonathan started to rinse off the soapsuds. 'It's my mother's idea. The school sent me home, because I have nightmares and keep 'em all awake, so she's palmed me off on your father who's going to work me so hard I won't have the strength to work up any more nightmares.'

'I say, good wheeze, eh? You're here to stay? You're going to live here? That's great! What do you have nightmares about, for heaven's sake? Your mother?'

Jonathan grinned and didn't answer.

Peter said, 'I'm all for it. If you've got the job, I haven't got three hunters to plait before school tomorrow.'

'Yes, you have. I've never plaited in my life.'

'We'll soon change that. Tomorrow, to be exact.'

'I think I've finished now, with this mare—'

'You're going to stay and help me do evening feeds and bed them down? Cripes, you can't knock off just when I get home. There's no justice—'

'I don't know what they arranged.'

Peter re-arranged it, whatever it was. 'If he's going to plait tomorrow morning,' he explained very reasonably to his father, 'he wants to be here at six, so he might as well stay the night right from now, mightn't he? Then he can help me with evening stables as well.'

'Suits me,' said McNair.

'He can have the spare bed in my room. It'll take more than a few screams from him to keep me awake.'

Jonathan was already thinking that, if he sat down, he would fall asleep immediately. The house was warm and steamy with cooking, and chaotic underfoot with Giovanni and his plastic toys and a pair of spaniels and wet anoraks thrown down and left. Mrs McNair was standing at the cooker singing. Mr McNair was in a small untidy office doing his books. The rooms in the house were well-used, with the paint chipped round the door frames and the tiles cracked in the hearth, the chair arms beginning to sprout stuffing; it seemed to Jonathan busy and cramped after the cool acres of their big, perfect rooms at home. But it was very comforting to him, coming in with his hands raw from the cold water, his thigh muscles stiffening already from the hours of trotting, his mind a blank. He said little, ate a large meal, did the evening stables with Peter, had a hot bath and fell asleep in front of the television. Mrs McNair, having informed Mrs Meredith of the change of plan, chivvied him to bed, and he slept instantly, sprawled on his face under a yellow horse-blanket on a sagging divan. Peter, coming up an hour later, wound up his alarm which was set perennially for five forty-five, and put it close to Jonathan's bed-head.

'Sweet dreams, matey,' he muttered, and joined him in oblivion.

'If you had a nightmare last night, nobody heard you,' he declared the following morning, setting out his plaiting kit on the windowsill of one of the hunters' loose-boxes. Jonathan, yawning, tied the gelding up short and started to comb out its mane. When it was done he combed his own hair with the mane-comb.

'I didn't.'

'Divide it into nine, and keep me supplied with thread in the needle. You can do Paddy when you've seen how it goes.'

Peter got a bucket to stand on and started work. He was very deft and quick, his fingers neat as a girl's. He frowned slightly as he worked, his breath making a cold cloud round his face.

'You supposed to be ill or something?' he asked. 'I mean, mental?'

'Yeah. They sent me here to the nut-house.'

'Seriously, what are the nightmares about?'

'Oh, what happened . . . getting shut up . . .'

'But it won't happen again. What's the worry?'

Jonathan passed up the needle and waited while he fastened the first plait. And the scissors. Peter started on the next. Jonathan said, slowly, 'I think it's because I've got a conscience about it all being rather my fault, my parents losing all that money.'

'How can you think that?'

'My mother thinks so. I'm sure of it.'

'She never said so?'

'No, not exactly. I might have it wrong, I suppose, but she gives me that feeling. And she's obsessed with getting them caught. I think that's why she's staying in Switzerland—doing her own sleuthing.'

'I can understand her feeling like that.'

'Yes. It's a lousy crime, kidnapping.'

'And the fact they're playboy types—got quite a pile already. No wonder she's mad. I'd feel the same.'

'Yes. But it's not very nice to live with. Her being like that, and me knowing it was partly my fault.'

'Why do you say that?'

Jonathan was re-threading the needle, and concentrated on it very hard. 'I might have tried more, at the end, to attract attention. They could have been caught, perhaps, if I'd done the right things. But I was too bloody scared.'

'Anyone would've been.'

'Tell my mother that.'

'Yeah, I get your point. Catch the bastards yourself then, and prove yourself a hero.'

Jonathan grinned. 'The solution, in a nutshell.' He handed the scissors. Peter cut off the thread and combed out the mane still to be done, considering the divisions. He said, 'The police don't seem to be bothering very much, although they worked hard enough while you were missing. They haven't followed up the home end—I mean, who was the person I met, on Mrs Allsop's hunter? They haven't followed that up at all.'

'And Jamie,' Jonathan said.

'Who's Jamie?'

'The bloke employed to watch me. I reckon he was a local. He knew Florestan. I think he was a groom, or something similar. He was Irish and he knew horses.'

'What's he look like?'

'How should I know? I never saw him. I would recognize his voice though. But how would it help, to track them down? I daresay they were just paid to do their bit, and that's it. What we want to know is exactly where John, Paul, and Ringo are now.'

'It's quite likely a couple like that would know, don't you think? The one I met was a well-educated bloke, a good friend, probably. He must know what their plans were. Even your Jamie—he might have heard quite a bit about where they were intending to go. He was very much involved, surely? Pretty guilty, I should say. He helped bash you about, and if they'd chucked you overboard he would have been an accessory, surely?'

'Yes, it would have taken all four of them, I'm sure, to do that.'

'Do you think they really would have?'

'I did then. I don't know what I think now. The whole thing seems pretty unbelievable, now.'

'Yes, but it happened.'

'Jeez, yes, it happened.' Jonathan could not help a shiver running through him, the morning being so raw and the memories chilling.

'We could do a bit of sleuthing on the side, see if we can find Jamie or our midnight rider,' Peter said. 'They're local, by the sound of it, and horsey. So what better chance, out hunting, or when the point-to-points start? How long are you going to be here?'

'My mother wants me to race Florestan. She said till the spring, if I wanted.'

'Do you want?' Peter looked down from his bucket, his face very interested.

Jonathan shrugged. 'I don't know.'

'If you stay,' Peter said, 'it would be terrific—I mean, if you've got Florestan to qualify, and I've got Garnet, we

122

can spend half our time till Christmas out hunting. And then afterwards, racing—it would be great, the two of us. Far more fun than just me on my own. I've got to do it anyway.'

'What about school?'

'Oh, I'm not there half the time now. I've gone sixteen. Officially I can't leave till Easter but I don't see that they'll bother.'

'I've got to go back, but I'm in no hurry, the way I feel. If you're going to be around too, it might be quite nice. Especially the hunting and racing. I'm not so keen on all this sort of lark though.'

'No, well, that's because you're a spoilt rich beast, used to having your own groom at home. It's time you learnt how the other half lived, Meredith. It'll make a man of you. Say you'll race Florestan—tell your ma—and then I'll stay at home too and work here with you. It'll be okay. I was going to try and get a job somewhere else, otherwise, and my old man doesn't like that idea. So it'll postpone a family row.'

'Why, doesn't he pay you?'

'No. Is he paying you?'

'I think so. It's not supposed to be a favour, my being here.'

'Well, he can bloody well pay me too, if I'm going to stay and work all day as well as all night, like now. We'll have a good time, Meredith, the two of us, especially the racing. And a bit of sleuthing too. What do you say?'

'Yes, suits me.'

'Okay. You go and plait Paddy then, I'll do the mare, and I'll go to school till Friday, then call it a day. Start work here on Saturday.'

The idea of having Peter as companion in his new gruelling life appealed to Jonathan considerably. The work-force at McNair's was not exactly congenial, consisting of old George, who didn't believe in talking, Maggie, a strong, stringy female of indeterminate age, bluff and downright in manner, pleasant enough but not exactly on his wavelength, and two rather secretive, terribly horsey girls called Jill and Sandra, who embarrassed him with their looks and giggling. Peter would balance the genders nicely and make the job a lot less boring.

By the time he had plaited half Paddy's mane and Peter had come to finish him off, he was nicely awake, warm and hopeful, which he hadn't been an hour earlier. With Peter he mucked out about a dozen loose-boxes, then Peter said he would have to go in for breakfast because of school.

'You come too,' he said. 'Privilege. Next week we'll start properly and have breakfast later, when all the horses are done.'

By done, he meant mucked out and fed, which took about an hour and a half. The system went into action the following Saturday: they got up at seven, worked, and went into breakfast at half-past eight. By the time they went back to the yard the girls had come, and the rest of the day was spent in grooming, exercising, and schooling. The girls went home at six, leaving them to feed, with George, and bed down. It was a twelve hour day, and Jonathan never had another nightmare.

11

Quite honestly, Elizabeth, I don't know what I'd do without him if you send him back to school now,' Mr McNair said, somewhat peevishly, on the telephone. 'I thought you wanted him to ride Florestan in his races? The first race is only five weeks away now, and he's put an awful lot of work in on the horse.'

'It was only meant as a temporary arrangement, Arthur. The school has been enquiring as to what we're up to, you see, and now we're back from Switzerland—well, I've got to make up my mind. I must say, though, I'd like him to see Florestan through the racing season. It's always been my wish to get Jonathan racing.'

'I'll tell you one thing, my girl, it would be more than our job's worth to put the two boys in the same race—'

'What do you mean, Arthur? You mean Jonathan and Peter?'

'Yes. Working together like this—well, your boy's good, Elizabeth, although he hasn't had as much experience as Peter, and they're very competitive. Very sharp together—I have to watch them sometimes, else they'll race when they're just supposed to be having a pipe-opener. They're very evenly matched, the two horses, you know—it's uncanny. Your Florestan and my Garnet. It'll be very interesting to see how they go—'

'Really? I never thought Jonathan was competitive at all! It must be your influence, Arthur. I shall have to come and see.'

'Yes, come round for a drink. It's nice to have you back again—as long as you don't want that boy of yours. Any news from the police, or have they given up? Do they still think those rogues are in Switzerland?'

'They're said to have moved on, but nobody has a clue as to where. Interpol just isn't interested. I feel very depressed, coming away and not one jot of progress. I still feel just the same about the whole thing, no less bitter. But it's no good dwelling on it, I suppose.'

'No. We seem to have forgotten it at this end. No word at all from the police here—well, not to us. But it doesn't mean to say they're not working on it.'

'I'm glad you think so, Arthur. I'll think it over about Jonathan staying with you until the spring. If he's very keen to race, why not, eh? See what he says.'

'Yes, dear, will do.'

Jonathan was a lot keener to race than go back to school.

'I've done all the bloody work on that nag, to get it fit. I don't see why I shouldn't have the fun too, as a reward.'

School, somehow, seemed far away. Jonathan, cured of nightmares, wasn't cured of his uncertainties, nor his guilt complexes. Making good at racing was going to be his way of *showing* his mother . . . he didn't want it to be like that, but it just was. When racing was over, in the spring, for better or for worse, he would go back to school and his old ways. Being at McNair's was just an interlude, a therapy spell. Because of Peter, it was all right; he liked it. Without Peter, it would have been bearable, but deadly boring. Horses were a colossal chore, unless one was totally committed, needing non-stop care and attention, day in, day out.

'It's your upbringing,' Peter complained. 'You're used to having everything done for you. It's been very bad for you, Meredith. What do you want to be when you grow up, Meredith—should that day ever come? A Tory MP? A marriage guidance counsellor? A—'

'Very funny. I'm going to be a tycoon, like my father.'

'Honestly?'

'I would be happy if I could do what my father has done, yes.'

'But he's already done it.'

'Yes, but it goes on all the time. You can't stop and rest on your laurels.'

'Do you really want to do that sort of thing?'

'Yes, I think so. It's fascinating—taking risks, playing a hunch, trying to work out what the other party is up to . . . I like figures, and facts. I'm not really a very physical sort of bloke.'

'Well, for an intellectual, you're a passable groom.'

'If I could really have my way, I'd stay here till Easter, win every race I'm entered for, round up those crooks single-handed and deliver them to my mother to shut her up, go back to school and get A's for every subject, leave and do economics and some practical accountancy, I think, and then join my father and beat him at his own game.'

'Very modest, my boy.'

Jonathan grinned. 'Yes, and out of that lot, I think shutting my mother up comes top of the list.'

'I think if you win on Florestan she'll take you back to her bosom with cries of delight.'

Jonathan thought so too. But he was only a beginner; it was optimistic to think about winning. This would be Peter's first year too, but he had all the time in the world, having decided to make it his career—Jonathan knew he only had till Easter.

'Lucky it's a good horse—it'll need to be,' he said.

They were riding knee to knee along one of the home

lanes at the time and an open gateway was coming up which gave into an empty cow pasture. Jonathan saw Peter notice that the gate was open and the cows gone, grinned, and waited for the suggestion.

'Shall we—?'

'Yes, of course.'

They turned in and the two big horses, knowing, hauled for their heads. It was possible to hold them, but difficult. Both the horses were goers, needing no prompting at all, and the boys, being of a like mind, had done little to discourage their exuberance. As Peter said, crouching over Garnet's withers and screwing his eyes up against the cold wind, 'This is what they're *for.*' He was perhaps convincing himself, knowing that his father wouldn't have entirely approved of the way they rode, but when the grass was there, and nothing but space in front . . . well, good resolutions weren't everything. Jonathan sometimes had slight qualms about what his mother would think when she came to ride Florestan again herself, but that day was not imminent. Meanwhile, always, they started with good intentions, a good collected canter, keeping side by side. But . . .

Peter said, turning his head, 'Your horse is going too bloody fast.'

Jonathan said, 'How come you're still with me then?'

'I'm not going to let a public-school nit like you get in front of me.'

'No? I haven't noticed.'

'I'm going to jump the hedge at the bottom.'

Jonathan lifted his head and surveyed the prospect, not with great enthusiasm. He hadn't very long to make a decision.

'You sure there's no wire in it?'

'Yeah. Big ditch the other side though.'

'You mean it?'

'Yes.'

Oh, well, Jonathan thought, what the hell? Mummy couldn't get much crosser, even if he killed her precious horse. The hedge wasn't a doctored racing fence, but a nasty prospect of old hawthorn and overhanging elm trees. He chose his place, glanced at Garnet to see that he wasn't making for the same spot, used all his strength to channel Florestan's wild impulsion into a strong, considered take-off, and prayed. Florestan stood well back like the good horse he was and sailed over. It was terrific: frightening and fantastic all together, the jump huge, and the satisfaction as great. He knew he had ridden the horse well. Credit wasn't all for the nag: a goodly bit was for him. It made him feel very impatient for the actual racing.

Peter was pulling back into a canter, turning to see if Florestan was still there, grinning again. They continued fairly fast in a circle back to the road, jumped a much smaller hedge and rail back on to a handy grass verge, and pulled up, splattering mud and sweat.

'Cripes, they'll never believe we've only been walking and trotting—' Peter broke into song, a spirited rendering of the ancient 'They'll never believe me,' and they made the horses walk quietly the rest of the way home.

Racing started in the middle of February. The first race he went in for, Jonathan was fourth. His parents weren't there, and he was glad, for the whole thing was a jumble and a mess in his mind. He did nothing really wrong, but he was too green to know properly what he was doing. On form, Florestan should have come at least third, and possibly, properly ridden, second. He ran well enough, but Jonathan knew he hadn't helped him very much; he had been nervous and over-anxious. Peter, in another race, was also fourth, but this was considered very promising, for Garnet had never raced before.

When they boxed the horses up to go home they were both tired and slightly irritable. George, who was supposed to be acting groom as well as driver, had disappeared into the beer tent, and Jonathan had to walk Garnet round to cool him off while Peter was changing. His mind mostly blank, he noticed a horse go past which—for no reason he could think of—reminded him of the kidnapping incident. He was puzzled, trying to work out the connection, but it didn't come to him until he had tied Garnet up and was starting to bandage his legs for the journey home. When Peter got back, pleased to find Jonathan had done all the chores, he found him in a state of considerable excitement.

'You know what we said—about doing a bit of sleuthing at the races—'

'Yes. What have you sleuthed?'

'Well, it might be a coincidence, I suppose, but a horse went past wearing three yellow bandages and one white one—the point being that my blindfold was a yellow horse bandage. Not all that common a colour for bandages, wouldn't you agree? And one missing—very interesting, I thought.'

'Yes! A clue quite possibly. Which horse?'

'Well, I don't know. It didn't dawn on me all at once, and by the time it clicked, no sign of horse. I thought perhaps its groom might be my Jamie.'

'Quite likely. Can't we look for him?'

'We could if we get Garnet boxed up. But remember, Jamie will recognize me, and I've no idea what he looks like.'

'You finish Garnet off then, and I'll have a snoop round for yellow bandages. What was he doing? Just walking round?'

'Yes, hadn't raced, by the look of him. So he's probably unbandaged by now—might be in the paddock. It was a bay.'

But without the bandages, seventy per cent of the horses were bay. Jonathan hadn't looked hard enough. They couldn't find the yellow bandages again.

'Might if we wait until the end,' Peter said, but they couldn't, because George was wanting to go, and they had to go with him to work at the other end. Mr McNair, having advised them, cheered them, and bawled them out for not doing better, was socializing in the owners' marquee and not likely to surface for some time. They decided to say nothing about the yellow bandages.

'We'll look again next week,' Peter said. 'They'll be the same lot of horses for the most part.'

'I'd know Jamie by his voice, nothing else.'

Jonathan felt restless and on edge, keyed up by the race, and worried by what he thought of as his failure. It was all right for Peter, on a horse that didn't know anything, but Florestan was an old hand, he should have done better. Perhaps next week he would. He must. He didn't feel like talking, sitting jammed in the steamy cab between Peter and George. Peter, although it was his first race too, was not excited; in fact, looked positively bored. Certainly he was used to competition; Jonathan supposed that taking Sirius to Wembley had been far more difficult than anything he had done so far with Garnet, and even that—coming second—he had taken very much in his stride. He was sickeningly professional, Jonathan thought, enviously—and was glad they weren't likely to have to race against each other.

'Where did Dad say it is next week?' Peter asked George. 'Sheppey Hill, is it? Or Pottenham?'

'Sheppey Hill.'

'All up and down and round and round,' Peter remarked. 'Corners like a Grand Prix course. Very unpopular, I understand.'

Jonathan said dubiously, 'You trying to put me off?'

'What, you on your supercharged, one-and-a-half litre job? Why should you be put off? You just have to steer well, that's all, otherwise you hurtle off course into a crowd of spectators.'

'Oh, thank you very much.' As if there wasn't enough to think about . . .

But Mr McNair seemed to think he had acquitted himself quite well, and Peter too, and Jonathan finished the day with a distinct impatience for Sheppey Hill.

A few days later, on an afternoon of lowering skies and bitter wind, Mr McNair drove them over to Sheppey Hill so that they could both walk round the course and see what to expect.

'The other jocks have done it dozens of times, but this is tricky first time round—it won't be wasting your time.'

No, Jonathan thought, hunched well down into the fur lining of his anorak, it does no harm to know where you're going, even if—come the day—you can't see for mud and flying tails and general incompetence. The landscape was empty as Siberia, and about as comforting. The course was two miles long and it was twice round and a half-mile uphill run to the last fence and the finishing post. It was mainly a natural course, unlike most of the others, with the fences actually over the hedgerows, although much doctored to make them stiff and safe, and some of the turns, as Peter had prophesied, were very sharp for a horse out of control.

'You can't afford to be out of control, of course,' as Mr McNair so rightly said. 'Not here. Good riding counts here. Keep your horse balanced all the time, and particularly round the bends, or—in this mud—you'll go down.'

Strange, now, with rain on the wind and sour grass spooked by gusts like wind on water, stretching bare and brown to the sepia woods and leaden clouds, rooks like blots wheeling and spreading on the water-colour sky—to picture it scrawling with racegoers and their clamour in two days time. It would be different enough then, Jonathan thought, shivering in silks and white breeches down at the start, waiting to take on Siberia and all its perils. They stood staring morosely at a fence as black and forbidding as prison walls, and Peter said, 'It'll look better from sixteen hands up,' but Jonathan was not convinced. Better, perhaps, not to see too well what was ahead: a little confusion might anaesthetize the nastiest qualms. But it wasn't the doing that frightened him, only doing it well enough.

'You worry too much,' Peter said, correctly. 'You'll never make Prime Minister before the ulcers get you.'

'No, I might not put up for it after all.'

But even Peter was unable to accept the setbacks of the following Saturday with complete equanimity. Halfway to Sheppey Hill the horsebox broke down. They were on an obscure road miles from any help and by the time George had doctored the inner works they had lost nearly an hour.

'That's my race,' Peter was moaning. 'I might as bloody well go home now.'

'Your father'll get you in another. Don't you worry.'

Jonathan didn't see the consequences immediately, only when Mr McNair met them on the course.

'I'll declare him for the Adjacent Hunts, then—that's the only solution. He's not ready for the Open. I can declare them together. Lucky you weren't any later.'

'We're in the same race, you mean?' Jonathan said.

'Yes, can't be helped, I'm afraid. And you haven't a lot of time to get ready. You'd better collect your gear and

133

go and get weighed in. I saw your old groom, Jim, in the beer tent, Jonathan—I'll go and collar him to help us. George can't do it on his own.'

Jonathan was thrown by the thought of racing with Peter. On form he should beat him, and he was afraid he wouldn't. It made the whole thing that much more personal, and it was too much that way already. He wanted to be cool and careless like a professional, but he was all screwed up. But Peter too was quiet and scowling. They walked across to the paddock in silence, pushing through the crowd. The first horse was already being led in. Jonathan's parents were outside the Committee tent and came across to greet them, looking very much like owners, he thought critically, in tweed and expensive leather, carrying shooting-sticks. His mother, curiously, looked younger and—could it be true?—prettier than usual. She kissed him and said, 'It's lovely to have someone to do it for me, so much more restful! I shall really enjoy myself today. Arthur says you both did well last week. I'm so sorry we had to miss it.'

'How do you like being a jockey then?' his father asked.

'I'll tell you after the race.'

'Very wise.'

They escaped into the changing tent, into the flapping gloom peopled by leathery, half-familiar faces, where, although kindly received and even encouraged with well-intentioned banter, Jonathan felt as if in a foreign land. Most of the men were twice or three times their age and looked every bit of it. It was very cold and a fair amount of long woollen underwear was in evidence. Jonathan laid out his racing clothes and started to strip off his anorak and jersey and fuggy old jeans, shivering. It was really impossible to answer his father's question; if he won he would like being a jockey, but if he was an also-ran—what then? He wished it didn't matter so much, then he could enjoy it more. But nobody *said* it mattered. It was only how it seemed to him, as if he had to prove himself. But he had never bothered before. Before what? Before being kidnapped. Besides making his mother so mad, Peregrine Corder and his friends had undermined something essential to his mental well-being. Jonathan, halfway into his racing breeches, paused to consider this revelation.

'We're in the next race, not the one after,' Peter said, quite kindly. 'Everyone else has weighed in but us.'

He was standing waiting, all ready, with saddle and weightcloth, looking perfectly self-possessed.

'I'm coming,' Jonathan said, and zipped himself up and reached for his crash-helmet. Meditations would have to come later. With luck he might be in a better frame of mind when he got back to the tent. He weighed out, and put his anorak on again, and they went out to the paddock together to meet their respective owners— which was the worst bit, Jonathan had already decided, being so public, and feeling so shivery and apprehensive. Once on board, everything took on a more hopeful perspective.

Jim, presumably summoned from the beer tent by Mr McNair, was still leading Florestan round, and Jonathan stood watching, comparing him with the opposition, fastening up the strap of his helmet. His parents were talking to the McNairs and some friends of theirs; bookies were still bawling the prices and the crowd pressed eagerly round the chestnut palings to make their last assessments. There were eleven runners, enough to make for a bit of excitement at the first fence. Jonathan moved out of the way as a large bay, brought in to be saddled, circled business-like quarters in his direction. Its groom checked it and started to strip off its rug, saying, 'Sure, you stupid old bastard, it's no time to be kicking up a fuss now—

you know what it's all about, you sorry old nag, you old cow, you . . .'

The voice, gentle and rhythmic, struck a chord in Jonathan. He instinctively shut his eyes, and knew it was Jamie.

'Sure, sir, he'll give you a fine ride. The ground's to his liking.'

Jonathan moved again, to get a look at the man, and saw a large, stocky, sandy-haired figure in a flat cap and brown overall holding the horse while its jockey girthed it up. The two of them were alone with the horse, and preoccupied with what they were doing. Jonathan, watching Jamie, had a powerful, angry knowledge that the man *knew* him: he knew the very bottom of his nature, the scraping of his soul's barrel; it made him sick. And while he watched him, scowling, Jamie suddenly looked up, almost as if he could sense the antagonism, and met Jonathan's gaze. His big, bland face—he was quite young, only in his early twenties—seemed to freeze over; then, very quickly he turned away and gave his jockey a leg-up.

'Jonathan, have you gone to sleep? Where's your saddle?'

Jonathan, shaken, turned back to his own horse, and saw its great, hard, gleaming, powerful muscles all bunched up with anticipation right beside him, his mother's face, tight and nagging suddenly, and his father's expression, curious and sympathetic. He handed up the weight-cloth and the saddle and scooped under Florestan's belly for the girth, not saying anything, while his mother tried to keep Florestan still. The horse, excited, wheeled about. Jonathan struggled with the girth buckles. His father said, 'Is anything the matter?'

Jonathan, straightening up, heard the question and saw Jamie watching them. He was very close to them,

136

Florestan in his dancing about having barged quarters with Jamie's bay, and Jonathan saw that Jamie wasn't intrepid and tough and clever like Peregrine Corder, but scared stiff.

'No,' he said to his father. 'Nothing's the matter.'

He took his anorak off and his father took it. Jim gave him a leg-up and he settled himself in the saddle, hitching his legs up into the short stirrups, feeling Florestan bunched beneath him with cold and excitement like a time-bomb ticking down to explosion time. It was all right now, no fear at all, not for anything, only a sort of numb area about Jamie, like shock, not knowing how to cope with it. But it would have to wait.

'I don't know what you've done to this horse,' his mother was saying, trying to hold on to Florestan's head. 'He was never so excitable when I rode him.'

'You can let go,' Jonathan said. 'He's all right.'

'Very well. Good luck then.' She looked worried stiff.

'My money's on you,' Jim said. 'Don't let me down. The horse looks a treat.'

'Yes, Jonathan, he's a picture. The best of luck!' His father waved his race-card, and Jonathan smiled and headed Florestan for the opening out of the paddock to follow the rest of the horses to the start. The horse was pulling like a train, nearly heaving him out of the saddle, his hindquarters dancing up and down like a yo-yo. They passed the end of the line of bookies and he saw that he was fourth on the list: there were two very good horses, Jackpot and Golden Wedding, which he knew he didn't stand a chance of beating, barring accidents, but he knew that if Florestan had sported a more experienced jockey, he would have been third favourite, not fourth.

'We'll show 'em,' he said to the horse. 'Bloody nerve, putting us down there!'

At last he was on the course and could let go, bucketing away the quarter-mile down to the start, past the jump that was both first and last and away from the crowds, feeling the icy wind of Siberia striking through his silk shirt and making his eyes sting and his nose run, seeing the brown grass stream away beneath him so fast it was as if he were in an aeroplane taking off. But the race hadn't started yet. He hauled back on the great mad horse, holding him, and saw the starter with his flag, waiting, laughing, and all the gaudy knots of people collected round the start. He cantered past and through the other horses and then pulled up and turned round, coming back at a walk, ready to answer the roll-call. Peter was already there on Garnet, walking round, looking very grim and professional, and Jonathan suddenly felt that now, racing against each other, they weren't really friends any more. Peter had always been like that in competitions: he was always very serious about winning; it wasn't just fun. Up to now, Jonathan had never bothered, but now he knew it wasn't fun either. He desperately wanted to do well, and he certainly wanted to beat Peter. He rode over to Peter and they walked round together, but Peter didn't say anything, or even smile. They had all answered to their names and the white flag was up. The starter shouted, 'Let's have you then! Make a line! Let's have a nice line!'

A horse barged Florestan and Jonathan had to turn him. There was a flurry of hooves and a humped back somewhere near the rails, but Jonathan got back next to Peter and they stood for a moment together, pulled up, waiting, because the two horses were in the right place. Jonathan, glancing back, suddenly saw Jamie's horse, and realized that he hadn't said anything, and he had a quick desperate vision of himself falling and getting trampled underfoot, and nobody knowing about Jamie, and he said very quickly to Peter, just as they started to move forward,

138

'Number eight is Jamie's horse.' Peter jerked his head round in surprise.

'Palm Court? You sure?'

'Yes.'

The other horses were moving up; they were all in a line now, surging forward knee to knee with the inevitability of a breaking wave, held only by the starter's upraised arm. It was a terrible moment, like the instant of deciding to go on the highest diving board, the fragile, dreadful fraction of a second before it all started to happen—then the flag dropped and the wave broke, and anything one might have been thinking about one's prospects, Jamie and Peregrine Corder, or any other damned thing under the sun, was all broken into fragments: a great lurch of panic in Jonathan's case and a blinding faceful of mud and then amazement to be going so fast, sitting there like a passenger looking out of a train window at the flying hedges—but hemmed in helplessly by a tide of straining, snorting horseflesh. What did one do? And, God Almighty, here was the first fence! Was it possible? The horse beside him hit it hard and Jonathan went over not quite sure whether the noise of rending brush might be caused by Florestan—for certainly he had done nothing to help the poor beast. But the feel of it was splendid, the animal landing far out and catching up a whole length on the leaders. 'Whoopee!' Jonathan said happily, and then, remembering that his mother was watching, 'I must pull myself together.'

It was easier, now that the first fence had sorted them out somewhat. Jonathan was in about the middle of the field. Jackpot, Golden Wedding, Palm Court, a bright chestnut called Penny Wise and Peter—blast him—were in front. The chestnut was being ridden by a girl—blast her. Bloody girls should stay at home where they belonged, not get out on the racecourses, especially not get in front.

She deserved everything that was coming to her. Florestan, going very easily, caught her up and she grinned and yelled something at Jonathan, obviously enjoying herself, and he changed his mind a bit and wondered if she would grow up like his mother. She was very dashingly made-up, with lots of eye-shadow, the whole effect now slightly bizarre with splatterings of mud. Their two horses raked along side by side, both settling down now. Jonathan could feel Florestan, after the first mad rush, remembering what it was all about, that there was a long way to go, but he was very fit and strong and pulling hard to get up with the leaders. But Jonathan held him back, not wanting to get too close, because he preferred to be where he would get a good view of the jumps coming up. Too close and the mud was really flying. He did actually see the second jump and was ready for it, following Garnet who jumped too close and ploughed a nice hole through the top. This mistake cost Peter a few lengths and Jonathan found he had now exchanged the girl's company for Peter's. He wasn't nearly so pretty, but his temper had improved since the start, for he grinned at Jonathan and said, 'How's things?'

'Quite nicely, thank you. Who's that girl on the chestnut?'

'Melissa Jones, you mean? You fancy her?'

The next jump was approaching fast and Jonathan, aware that Florestan was thinking of having a race of his own with his old mate Garnet, concentrated on gathering him together and getting him right for the nasty obstacle—it had a wide ditch in front of it which would sort out any mistakes. Peter was being similarly careful, and two horses came up very fast on the inside of them and jumped it ahead of them. Florestan and Garnet took off exactly together and cleared it nicely, but Jonathan had to check Florestan sharply to avoid the horse in front

140

which had swerved on landing. This left him suddenly three places behind, covered in mud and very cross. Melissa Jones was also very close, her horse's nose close beside his knee. However much he fancied her, he didn't fancy her coming past, and he sent Florestan on a bit to show that he didn't intend to be an also-ran. It was all a bit of a mess now, his plan of campaign non-existent, but there was still a long way to go. As long as the horses in front didn't get too far away everything was well. By the time they had completed the first circuit Jamie's horse, Palm Court, had dropped back and Jonathan was beside Peter again, with four horses in front. Two of these were the favourites, but the other two had to be overtaken, according to Jonathan's reckoning, and nobody else must be allowed to come up, not even Melissa Jones. Florestan was still going nicely, but so was Garnet, pulling harder by the look of him; Peter was spotted with his lather, and was having a hard job to keep him balanced, frowning with the effort, and Jonathan knew that he was the better-off and likely to have more in hand later. Florestan, wise old bird, knew what was still to come, but Garnet wanted to win at every fence. Jonathan heard Peter swearing at him; at one fence he nearly had Peter off, pecking on landing, and Jonathan lost them both for some time. One of the horses ahead put his rider off at the next fence and ran off the course, and the one remaining which Jonathan knew he must beat ran out of steam rapidly and Jonathan went past without any difficulty. This left him with only Jackpot and Golden Wedding ahead, both opening up a fair lead and fighting it out between themselves. It was almost too good to be true.

Jonathan glanced behind to see how things were going. Peter was catching up again, and the female was two lengths behind him. Then there was a long gap of some ten or fifteen lengths, and three or four weary horses were no danger. He began to feel very excited, and not a little tired, and frightened of the responsibility—frightened too of Peter. Whatever happened—anything—he wasn't going to have that begger in front of him at the post.

All the horses had slowed by now for the heavy ground was gruelling and the two in front had set a very fast pace for the conditions. In fact their lead wasn't so great now; Jonathan was getting flicks of mud from their hooves. They were still out in the country but heading for home for the last time. There were two more jumps out in the meadows and then the last one in front of the crowd, only about two hundred yards from the post. The run in to this jump was uphill and gruelling, and there was a very sharp bend into the bottom of the hill which was demanding on a tired horse. Jonathan knew that the ride had been easy up till now; this was where one had to keep one's head and work and not make any mistakes. He felt very nervous and excited, sweating hot with the effort and icy cold in the wind, stirred by the distant shouting of the crowd and this awareness of being at crisis point. Almost anything could happen, but he was in with a chance.

It happened.

So quickly that Jonathan, blinking away tears caused by the cold wind, nearly missed it. Jackpot, jumping ahead of him, swerved on landing and cannoned violently across Golden Wedding, bringing him down. Jackpot's jockey went over his head and landed in a heap just where Florestan was aiming to jump. Jonathan's instinct was to pull up—then he remembered that nobody did, not racing, for heaven's sake—he wasn't in the Pony Club now!— and he drove on, trusting in the horse to avoid the jockey as best it could. It all happened so fast; it was like having a blow-out on a motorway. It was all happening before there was time to think what to do for the best. Florestan jumped big, landing well clear of the jockey, but the loose horse ran across him and Florestan swerved violently to avoid him, nearly putting Jonathan over the side. Jonathan, officially in charge, found he couldn't think fast enough, only enough to hold on. There was a succession of lurches and mud flying, the confounded Jackpot swerving about all over the place in a great tizzy at being on his own, but Jonathan managed to gather his wits together and swing Florestan sharply right-handed to get back on to the inside of the course.

'Get out of my bloody way!'

Peter, unimpeded, was coming through close to the ropes. Jonathan drove Florestan into place beside him and the two horses ran on together. The two boys looked at each other briefly, but said nothing. In those few seconds everything had changed, and Jonathan knew that—for one of them—it was going to be the win of a lifetime, and neither he nor Peter intended it for the other. They were no longer friends.

The crowd was screaming itself hoarse with excitement at this sudden change of fortune and the deadly duel they could see developing, the sort of finish that made the day, even if the bet had been on a horse that was twenty lengths back. All the people were running across the side of the hill towards the finish, and to the wings of the second-last jump which the horses were now approaching. Jonathan, aware of the dangers ahead, was also acutely conscious of the whole scene, the amazing turn of fortune that had sharpened the experience into a kaleidoscope of icy detail, even to the exact expression on Peter's face, making him a complete stranger. His eyes were unwavering on the jump ahead, screwed-up against the wind; his skin seemed stretched tight over the bones in a quite unfamiliar way, taut with concentration, streaked with mud, the jaw set, nostrils dilated; even his body, carved by the wind against the silk shirt into a bony shell, as if all spare flesh

143

had been discarded, had a determination about it that was formidable. Jonathan sensed this instinctively: the calibre of what he was up against. But while he, too, was watching the fast approaching jump and judging his stride and his distance, there was a whole area of his brain apart, amazed, positively goggling at what was happening.

Both the horses were tired now, but they were used to racing together and it was as if they were settling into an old feud. They came to the jump very fast and they both went over together stride for stride, as if locked together. Immediately on the other side was the sharp right-hand turn into the uphill finish, with the last jump on the very top of the hill. Peter landed and turned very fast, by beautiful riding, keeping close to the rails, but Jonathan swung out rather wider, not trying to emulate Peter because he didn't think he was good enough, but not losing much either. Perhaps half a length.

And now the race was on, to the bitter end, and Jonathan knew that he held the advantage. Peter, for all his formidable determination, was on a green horse who didn't know that, when the pinch came, it wasn't time to give in. Jonathan could see Garnet flagging and rolling slightly, and wondering why he wasn't getting a breather; but Florestan, who knew what it was all about, was doggedly finding strength for his last effort. Jonathan nursed him, and saw him come up to Garnet, saw his knee draw level with Peter's and stay there. He wasn't bothered about Peter's expression any longer. He had this magnificent, precarious sensation of utter glory, going past, inch by inch, riding his lovely, game horse with all the skill he could summon, lifted up by the waves of sound from the crowd, like the roaring of breakers on a beach.

Precarious, indeed . . . Jonathan knew it was going to happen the moment before it did, feeling Florestan's hesitation a stride out. He sat there, incredulous, and felt Florestan's strength unequal to the effort of the last jump. He took off, but went straight through the brush instead of over it, landing on his nose in a great spray of broken birch and pitching Jonathan in a complete somersault over his head. Jonathan landed on his back and saw the shadow of Garnet pass over him, saw Florestan scrabbling to his feet . . . he closed his fingers hard over the reins and dug his heels desperately into the soft ground as the horse tried to gallop on. Florestan pulled up, wheeling about, tried to go on again after Garnet, but was held hard. Jonathan, on his feet, gulping for breath, reached for the saddle and a handful of mane and flung himself like a maniac across the horse's back. Head-down, wriggling and flailing, he felt Florestan lurch into a canter beneath him while one leg was only holding over the horse's back by the grip of a hysterical ankle-bone. He dropped the reins and got both hands into Florestan's mane—thank God, unplaited— heaved his stomach over the pommel and managed to swing his weight across enough to slide his leg down over the far side. All this time—and it seemed like a century—Florestan was cantering on, and where the winning post was Jonathan had no idea. He could hear the crowd screaming and the thudding of hooves into the squelchy ground, but by the time he had sat up and gathered in his reins again, he was going down the hill on the other side.

Peter was coming back towards him, grinning, standing up in his stirrups. Jonathan could not speak to him, and not only because he was half-winded and had a faceful of mud. If he could have had his wish Peter would have dropped stone-dead into the grass, hit by a thunderbolt. But as it was Peter pulled Garnet up and sat down in his saddle, looking exactly like the idiot he was, wiped the sleeve of his shirt over his face and said, 'Good race, eh?'

'It could have been better,' Jonathan said shortly.

Melissa Jones was pulling up beside them. She said to Jonathan, 'You swine, getting back like that! I couldn't believe my luck, seeing you go, and then—'

She turned away to talk to someone, and Jonathan realized that there were a whole lot of people talking to him, but he didn't seem to be hearing anything. He tucked Florestan in behind Garnet to make for the saddling enclosure, saw his parents coming towards him, and wished he'd been knocked unconscious.

'Am I second?' he asked his mother.

'Yes, darling,' she said, in a voice like steel. 'It was fantastic.'

Yes, Jonathan thought, fantastic, but fantastic how? He ought to be where Peter was. It was no good trying to put on a smile and be a good loser, because he was past it. He was a bloody bad loser, as bad as his mother, who could smile and manage to look utterly vicious at the same time. Such clever manners were beyond him. He buried his head into Florestan's side, scrabbling at the girth buckles, dragged off his saddle and cloth and bolted for the tent, ducking all the arms and guffaws and exclamations.

It wasn't much better in there.

'The infants sweep the field, eh? And a spectacular bit of trick-riding thrown in for good measure.'

Jonathan, following Peter on the scales, cracked out what he hoped was a pleasant expression.

'You should go in for gymnastics,' someone said, 'like those flaming Russians. Get a gold medal, you would.'

'Your mother never went through the last fence like that—never. She always went over like a lady.'

'Twelve stone, okay. How much weight do you carry, lad?'

'One stone five ounces.'

'Yeah, the horse is used to a lady aboard. Makes a difference the extra weight, come the last fence.'

Melissa Jones, weighed out, took her helmet off to reveal a shining blonde head, and disappeared into the female changing quarters. Jonathan sat on the bench next to Peter, fagged out.

'What did your mum say?' Peter asked, grinning.

Jonathan swore.

'I was supposed to give Garnet an easy race,' Peter said. 'I've just remembered. I shall get blasted.'

'Not for *winning*!' Jonathan said.

'We didn't know he was that good, did we?'

'No.'

And you, Jonathan thought, but he wasn't going to say it. He dragged off his shirt and breeches and washed all the mud off him and changed into his ordinary clothes, taking as long as possible. He combed his hair. The thought of going back to do evening stables didn't appeal. He was fed up with horses. He didn't want to talk to anyone about the race, not go through it fence by fence with his mother, not think about what he had so nearly achieved, and missed. It was no good thinking that he had done well to get on again and get second, he should have won. He might never get that chance again. He just couldn't go and talk about it, not yet.

He picked up his things and went out of the tent and away down the field blindly, to get lost until he felt civilized again. He felt slightly stoned and a bit sick. A horsebox went by him towards the gate and he had to stand and wait for it. As it went past he glanced up and saw the driver's face. It was Jamie.

He had forgotten all about Jamie.

Seeing him gave him a jolt, all the other things coming back, even the nightmares. He stood there feeling at rock-bottom, pounded by failure. The horsebox went past him

and down the field to the gate where there was a bit of a
queue, and Jonathan walked down after it, intending to
get the number—although they could easily look up the
horse's owner on the race-card, and get the address. But
when he got to the horsebox he saw the groom's door in
the side of it and, completely on impulse, he opened it and
got in. As he closed it behind him the horsebox drove on
out into the road, and Jonathan felt merely relieved to be
travelling away from all the people he didn't want to talk
to. Talking to Jamie would be quite different.

12

Wherever Jamie lived, it was a long way. Jonathan checked out at intervals and recognized the general direction; otherwise, he sat on the floor, padded with straw and a horse-blanket, and wondered what on earth he was going to do at the other end. What he wanted to do was just talk with Jamie, and even then, he wasn't sure what about. His mind was in such a tangle about everything. He didn't know where he stood—even in the race, was he a failure not to have won, or pretty clever to have come second, considering the circumstances? And why did it all have to matter so much? Because he had lost his self-respect, he supposed, and Jamie had been a part of that miserable business, and it needed talking over somehow. But up to date there had been nobody to talk it over with, apart from the suggested psychiatrist. How thick Jamie could play the psychiatrist he had no idea. But at least he might find out something about Peregrine Corder and co., to help the police in their enquiries.

Anyway, what the hell? . . . it was better than going home to a post-mortem with mummy, and to suffer Peter's quiet, glowing satisfaction at close quarters, and jibes from McNair and George. He needed time to work up a shell.

He sat trying not to think about anything at all, aware that there was no going back, and that he had done a very foolish thing, to add to all the other debits of his behaviour. As the journey went on he grew stiffer and colder and more and more depressed, picking at bits of

149

straw with raw fingers, his hands sore from Florestan's pulling. He kept going back over the race in his mind, and all his mistakes, and feeling more and more nervous about confronting Jamie, and nothing made sense any more.

After about two hours the horsebox left the road and started bumping slowly down a farm track and Jonathan presumed they were nearly home. He could have jumped out now and called it a day, but—having been so stupid—there seemed no point in not seeing it through. But he felt very nervous now, not entirely sure that Jamie wouldn't do him a damage. And who else would there be at home? He was going to have difficulty explaining to complete strangers what he was doing in the horsebox.

The horsebox swung round, presumably through a gateway, and came to a halt. Jonathan peered through his pane of glass and saw a decrepit farmyard with hens picking about, and a straw-stack and a tractor, and no signs of life at all, apart from animal. He got to his feet and stood waiting, slightly breathless. Then he climbed over the partition and stood by the horse's head, and heard the bolts on the ramp being undone. He could feel his heart pounding with fear. It never occurred to him that Jamie might be as frightened as he was.

They stood staring at each other. Jamie went white and his mouth fell open and his voice wouldn't work properly.

'What—what—oh, cripes, what are you—?' He cleared his throat. Jonathan heard the trembling in his voice. He couldn't think of anything to say.

'What do you want?' Jamie asked, with a great effort to get the words out.

Jonathan shrugged. 'I just—I don't know—just talk to you—'

'You're alone? Does anybody know you're here? Do they know—did you tell them—?'

'No. Nobody knows. I just came on an impulse.'

'On your own?'

'Yes.'

He looked relieved, and came up the ramp slowly, very suspicious.

'What have we got to talk about then? I'm not much interested in talking.'

Jonathan unfastened the horse for him, being near its head. 'Shall I bring him out?'

'Yes, if you want a job. I'm on my own here.' He moved back as Jonathan turned the horse round, and said, 'I only did that—what I did to you—under orders, like. I didn't get anything out of it. I worked as a groom for Mr Corder then, he asked me to go along. I didn't know what it was all about until it was too late.'

Jonathan didn't believe that, but said nothing, leading the horse carefully down the ramp into the dusking, muddy yard.

'Over there,' Jamie said, pointing to a loose-box in the corner of the yard. 'I'll go and put the light on, and get his rugs, if you take him.'

Jonathan led the horse across the yard. The light came on in the loose-box and showed it all ready for the night, fresh straw down and a hay net and water buckets filled ready. Jonathan, by force of habit, tied up the horse and started to undo its bandages. It was very quiet, wherever they were, no sound of traffic, only the purring of a cat that jumped in over the half-door and rubbed itself against Jonathan's legs, and the munching of the horse at the hay. It was raining softly, and the water was trickling out of holes in the gutters and splashing in a homely way on the concrete outside. Jonathan knelt in the straw and massaged the horse's legs with his cold hands, wondering what on earth he had got himself into.

Jamie came back into the box with the horse's night-rugs. He put them in the manger, and stood there with a gun in his hand. Jonathan looked at it, and looked at Jamie and said, 'I don't see what you want that for. I haven't come here to do you any harm.'

'No, I daresay. But it won't hurt you to know I've got it, will it? And I know how to use it too.'

It seemed very unreal, suddenly. Jonathan had never seen a gun before, out of a film, except for rabbits and pheasants. But he didn't find it particularly frightening.

'Have you ever used it?'

'I killed somebody once,' Jamie said. There was a slight edge of pride in his voice. 'That's why I left home and came to this lousy country.'

'From Ireland you mean?'

'Yes. It's not safe for me over there, else I'd be back. I'm a peaceful man at heart, you know. I don't want trouble.'

'No, nor me.'

'As long as you haven't got the police on me or anything—it's just to show you, warn you, like.'

'No. It's okay. There's nothing like that.' Jonathan started to unbuckle the horse's rugs, to change them for the night rugs. 'Are you going to rub him down?'

'You can do it. I'll make him a feed.'

He fetched a box of grooming kit and put it handy, and Jonathan started on the job, thinking about the gun, trying to work out just how dangerous Jamie was. He certainly up to now had never thought of him as threatening. Even with the gun his image didn't change; he still looked homely and cloddish, his flat round face congenitally simple. When he came back with the horse's feed Jonathan asked, 'Is the gun loaded?'

'Yes, of course. Wouldn't be much good otherwise. It's a killer, that gun.'

Jonathan felt more optimistic, Jamie proving himself every minute more childlike. Now he had the gun he appeared far more friendly, as if having great faith in its ability to guard him. Jonathan became more optimistic about getting him to talk, especially if he was on his own in this lonely place. At the back of his mind it occurred to him that a dumb ox like Jamie might be more dangerous with a gun than a more intelligent man acutely aware of the consequences, but this thought he discarded as irrelevant—to his eternal regret, as he remembered a very long time afterwards. For an irrelevant thought, it was dead on target.

The horse plunged its nose into its feed and Jonathan, seeing that he was dry, if not very clean, said, 'You don't want to disturb him now he's feeding, do you? Shall I rug him up?'

'Okay.'

Jamie helped him, now quite amicable.

Jonathan asked, 'Whose is this animal? It's not one of Mr Corder's?'

'No. I don't work for him now, not since he went away. This isn't much of a job, just for a farmer—but I thought I'd better lie low for a bit, the police nosing around, you know. And it suits me—as long as I can get round the races.'

'It's a lonely spot.'

'Yes, very. Part of the attraction. There's no one here at weekends. The gov'nor generally comes to the races, but he's gone up North this weekend. I shan't see anyone now till Monday morning.'

Better and better, Jonathan thought. He buckled the surcingale and Jamie said, 'I'll put the kettle on, if you want a cup of tea. As long as you're up to no mischief, remember.'

'No.'

'I can't say that I wouldn't be glad of a bit more company sometimes. I'll show you where I live.'

There was a tack-room at the end of the row of buildings, quite a large one with a big stove glowing in one corner, and Jamie had a table and an armchair in it, and a cupboard with some food in. Some racing papers lay on the table, and a form-book, and there was a very old, smelly dog lying on a rug in front of the fire. It was surprisingly homely and comfortable, a large black kettle already gently steaming on the top of the stove. Jonathan realized that he was cold and tired and when Jamie gestured him to the armchair he sank into it with relief. The race had taken more out of him than he had realized; the blanket warmth of the fire was thick, almost tangible, a gorgeous comfort. Jamie put the gun on the table and took the hard upright chair to assert his authority. But his face was now entirely friendly. He made the tea very strong, and got a bottle of whisky out of the cupboard and topped the mugs up generously, and put a lot of sugar in.

'That how you like it, eh?'

'I shall go to sleep.'

'You rode a good race today. That your first?'

'Second.'

'You should've won. But not your fault—the extra weight told, I daresay. I had my money on you, you know.'

'Well, you lost it.'

'No, for a place. I cheered myself silly when you got on again like that. I've never seen anything like it—to pip that girl just on the post. She was coming up fast.'

'I never saw her.'

'Oh, it was splendid! Very neat. I bet your old ma was pleased.'

'I didn't notice.' Jonathan was surprised by Jamie's tribute, not having seen the finish in this light himself.

'And that McNair boy—he's a beautiful rider for such a babe. He'll go a long way, I'm thinking. On such a green horse—he didn't have an easy ride at all. Oh, I'm envious when I see riding like that.'

'Envious?'

'It's what I should've done—like to have done. Ridden them, I mean, not just led them round the parade ring.'

'Well, why not? Haven't you ever had the chance?'

'It's not just the chance.'

'What then?'

Jamie looked down into his tea-cup, his big red face clouding over. When he looked sullen, he looked more childlike than ever. He had taken his cap off, and his hair was sandy fair and baby fine, in wispy curling locks, adding to the effect. And yet he was a huge man of enormous strength. Jonathan remembered the effect of his great hands pushing him down into the life-raft case, like rock on the back of his neck—and yet now, faced with him, he seemed extraordinarily gentle.

'You need the guts. I haven't got the guts.'

Jonathan couldn't believe it. 'For that?'

'Of course.'

'But—' Jamie seemed to have turned everything upside down. 'I'm not—you, you of all people, should know—'

'Should know—?'

'If I can do it, of course you could too. You should know that I'm not—well, on that boat, you must remember—'

'I remember you fought like a tiger.'

'Not at the end. I didn't have any guts at all.'

'What do you mean? I don't remember.'

'At the end, when they said I had to go ashore in that life-raft case again—don't you remember? I cried, and I asked for those pills—so that I shouldn't know—'

'Oh, yes, but it was all over then. That was just sense.

You'd come through, hadn't you?—you'd fought them all the way, and you didn't say anything all that time, waiting for the message to come, and knowing what was going to happen if it didn't. I thought the whole thing had failed. And I was more frightened than you were, because I thought I'd got involved with a murder. And you—you were the one who was going to be murdered, yet you didn't show any fear at all. I've never forgotten that.'

Jamie seemed to remember it better than he did. He remembered how frightened *he* had been, yet he didn't remember Jonathan's grovelling performance at all.

'But afterwards, when they said I had to go in that case again—don't you remember?—' Jonathan desperately wanted Jamie to remember. 'I begged—I pleaded for those pills—'

'Yes, but it was all over then. You couldn't have done anything. It was just sense. Much better than being gagged, because we nearly killed you the first time—that was the gag—I thought you were suffocated, and so did the others. They were frantic, till you showed signs of life. Frightened? You never saw anyone more frightened than that lot when they opened the case!'

'Really?'

'I'm telling you, Corder had to take tranquillizers after you'd come round, to steady himself. He kept saying, "We've killed him and we haven't bloody started yet!" He was in a terrible state. And look at me. I just wanted to die, and that was only seasickness. The whole thing was a terrible experience—not worth the candle.'

He picked up the whisky bottle and filled his half-empty teacup with it, and then waved the bottle towards Jonathan.

'A drop more?'

Jonathan, thinking a celebration was in order, passed his cup over. He felt slightly intoxicated already, without any whisky, by Jamie's extraordinarily different picture of their days at sea.

'I thought you were a bloody marvel,' Jamie said. 'Corder did too. He said afterwards that he thought you were too good to murder, and if he'd had the wit to realize how much he would come to respect you he'd never have been so stupid to think that he could bump you off. It was all much more complicated than he had imagined—once feelings came into it. I mean, he did have feelings, funnily enough. Although he's a rogue through and through.'

Jonathan, sitting there with his whisky, tried to memorize what Jamie had just said. It started off, 'I thought you were a bloody marvel. Corder did too.' And then something about how much Corder had come to respect him, but he couldn't remember—only the word 'respect'. It was a reference, completely unsolicited; if only it was in writing, for his mother to read! And quite, quite different from his own view.

'What's happened to Corder? Do you ever hear from him?' The question was perfectly spontaneous, not loaded at all, although after he had asked it Jonathan realized that it was, really, the core of what his visit was all about. He had wanted to find out about Corder's whereabouts to please his mother and make up for being a failure, but now that motive was obsolete. He wasn't a failure.

'Well, I've told you, he's a rogue,' Jamie said roughly. 'He conned me into going on this trip—I didn't know what it was all about until it was too late, or I wouldn't have gone. I don't hold with kidnap—the trouble I got into at home now, that's different. I might have killed a man, but it was fair fighting, nothing underhand, you know—and I paid for it, by having to come away. But I'm not a villain at heart, not of Corder's kind, at least. It was a very dirty job he pulled. And some of us didn't get paid when it was all finished.'

'He came into enough. He could have afforded it.'

'Too right. What did I get out of it? I lost my job, because after he'd scarpered there wasn't a job, was there?—and I've had the police nosing around looking for me and I've had to keep quiet and lie low, like. I lost out all ways, didn't I? And there's he and his pals, living in the lap of luxury out in Aussie somewhere—it makes you sick.'

'Aussie? You mean Australia?'

'That's right. He even has the nerve to write to me, to ask me how his horses are running, even though they're sold up. Cocky little bastard. Says the money's on its way, but I'll believe it when I see it. Do you want to see the letter?'

'Yes.'

Jonathan couldn't believe his luck. Jamie had by now drunk a good deal of the whisky and was working up a grievance—quite understandably, if Corder had never rewarded him. And there had been no one else to talk it over with, until now. Jamie went to a drawer in the table and rooted out amongst a pile of racecards, and drew out a flimsy airmail letter. He tossed it to Jonathan.

'Read it for yourself! What a nerve!'

Jonathan looked at the address, but it was a P.O. Box number, and then a very long aboriginal name with lots of double OOs in it, ending with gong, and another one equally difficult underneath it.

'He's changed his name, of course, and being in the money trade for a living I suppose he knew how to sort out all that cash over there. I reckon you have to be very clever to win at his sort of game—you respect him, in a way—but then he should pay his debts. That's my grievance.'

'Has it ever occurred to you—this letter—how valuable it would be to the police? They're looking for him, after all.'

'But how could I go to the police? And what would I get out of it? I don't want their gratitude. I just want my money, that Corder owes me.'

'If you let me have this letter, I could guarantee that you would be paid the amount that Corder owes you, and that the police wouldn't bother you.'

'How could you do that?'

'It would be easy, surely? The police don't want you anyway—only for the lead you could give them on Corder, which is in this letter. And my parents would pay you for this information. I know they would—and a bonus too, I should imagine, if they get their money back.'

'How can I trust you?'

'You don't have to trust me. It's just common sense. You don't want this letter, do you? The police don't want you, I know that. They won't touch you. And I just know that my parents will reward you. How can you lose? You'll have some cash and be in the clear.'

'Well, I've no loyalty to Corder. If it's as you say—'

He poured some more whisky into his empty mug. 'I'd like a bit of cash to get on my way, go home perhaps. There's nothing for me here. That's why I thought, with Corder—well, some good might come out of it. Some more to drink?'

Jonathan got up and poured some of the stewed tea off the stove into his cup. At the same time he put the letter into the back pocket of his jeans, and passed the cup over for some more whisky. He didn't intend to drink it, but he wanted to keep Jamie humoured until he could gracefully retire. He wasn't sure how he was going to get home, but supposed he could find a phone box out along the road somewhere. He felt satisfied—deeply, incredibly happy, in fact, but not yet in a position to savour it fully; adjustment of this nature couldn't be instantaneous; it had to filter in slowly, over a fair period of time, and get digested. He didn't think he had got it wrong. He thought that probably he had just got it right. But he couldn't discuss it with anyone, because nobody had known what he had been suffering from all along, or even that he had been suffering at all. The instinct to follow Jamie had been right after all.

He thought if he sat down again he would fall asleep. But he could hardly, having got his information, tear out into the night without making a bit of an evening of it. Jamie was a lonely, bottled-up man, which is why he had talked so readily; he had needed remarkably little prompting.

'Is there a pub round here?' Jonathan sat on the arm of the chair with his recharged cup. 'Perhaps I could buy you a drink before I go home?'

'Aye, we could walk along a little later. It's down the road, half a mile. I've the calves to feed first.'

But he didn't seem in a hurry. He went on talking about his new guv'nor and the horses, and Jonathan sat trying to keep his eyelids from drooping. Half-dozing, he heard the sound of a car approaching, travelling very fast, the tyres slicing through the mud. He glanced out of the window and saw headlights swing in through the yard gateway, and another pair behind.

Jamie got up. Jonathan saw the look on his face, and ran to the door and opened it.

'You bastard!' Jamie screamed. 'You dirty, lying, double-crossing little bastard!'

He picked up the gun and fired. And fired again.

Jonathan knew he was done for, even before it happened. Just like the old television, he thought, seeing the police spilling out. But this time it was for real, including the gun. You never guessed, seeing it on film, that that's what it felt like—being shot in the back. It wasn't—entertaining—at all—

160

13

When Peter's alarm clock went off at five forty-five the next morning he got up as usual and went down to the stables. He had to, it being Sunday, and George's day off, and his father in such a state the night before . . . the horses didn't know anything was any different, after all, and were just as hungry and mucky as on any ordinary morning. That was the drawback with this job; it didn't allow for a change in the routine, a touch of flu, a death in the family . . . the horses didn't understand.

Without Jonathan, it took ages. Florestan and Garnet had to get some special attention, and would both need walking out later to stop them getting stiff. Thirty-odd horses needed feeding and the dung taken out. It took him till half-past nine, working methodically round the wet grey yard, not thinking about anything other than what he was doing, aware in his limbs of his hard race yesterday, aware in his brain of the awful thing that had happened but very carefully not thinking about it.

When he went indoors at last the house was unnaturally subdued and quiet. His stepmother cooked his breakfast and laid it on the table in silence, but kindly, looking at him anxiously.

'What's the news?' Peter asked. 'Have you rung up?'

'Your father rang up. What they say, Arthur? You tell him—'

'Oh, no change. Critical, they say, whatever that might mean. A critical condition. His parents are both over there.'

Peter sprinkled salt over his fried eggs.

'He's a great one for getting himself into trouble, that boy,' Mr McNair said heavily.

'Any news of Jamie?'

'No. He got clean away. The fog helped him.'

'It would have been better if I'd kept my mouth shut,' Peter said. 'If I hadn't said about Jamie.'

'Well, nobody knows what was going on, do they? He went missing, you guessed where he'd gone to, and so the police went to see. Why ever didn't he leave a message to say where he'd gone?'

'Because he was so fed up. He just wanted to disappear for a bit. He's like that, you know he is.'

'The police are at the hospital waiting to see if he can tell them anything. But it's not very hopeful apparently. He's been on the operating-table all night and isn't likely to come round for ages.'

'Ugh,' said Peter.

Poor old Jonathan, who didn't like being fussed over . . . for a very private person he was a genius at hitting the headlines. Even in his race, his spectacular bit of work over the finishing line had been the talk of the afternoon; if he'd stayed on a bit to hear, he'd have heard nothing but praises—even from grim old mother Meredith, once she'd got over the shock. But, being him, self-denigrating perfectionist that he was, he'd had to go off to probe old sores, the idiot!—and Melissa Jones, changed into a stunning red outfit that left no doubts at all as to the exact last half-millimetre of her vital statistics, asking, 'Who's that dreamy friend of yours, the one with the lovely black curls? I think he's smashing. Where's he sprung from?' . . . all to no avail. Don't die on us, Jonathan, and lose out on all your lovely opportunities—it's all starting for you, if only you knew it—

He couldn't see his bacon and eggs very well, feeling

162

shockingly emotional, but forced them down, chomping stolidly, positively glad that there were all those horses to groom and exercise and feed again, and muck out and bed down. It was deadly on his own, but just what he wanted, not to stay talking to anybody, or listening for the telephone, but just working himself into a stupor. He rode out on Garnet and then on Florestan, only walking, thinking back about the race and all its extraordinary turns of fortune, thinking that he was going to have two horses to ride until the end of the season; there was a tough time ahead, whatever happened, and things wouldn't ever be the same again.

In the evening, Mrs Meredith called in. She looked terrible, far worse than she had ever looked before.

'No, it's all just the same. No change. They can't say—won't commit themselves. There's no point staying on—you're just in the way. I can't see him, so I might just as well be at home in bed. I shall go out like a light, I know, and just pray that there's a turn for the better by morning.'

'Well, he's a tough lad—he's very fit. I daresay he'll pull through all right. You just get some sleep, my dear.'

But Mrs Meredith turned away from Peter's father and said to Peter, 'Why did he go there? Why did he do it, Peter? He must have told you?'

But Peter wouldn't tell her, although he knew perfectly well why Jonathan had gone. He wanted to say to her, 'If you'd just said, when he came back to the paddock, that he'd ridden a good race, and been pleased, he wouldn't have gone.' He shook his head. Of course, he had no idea if that was true; it was only what he felt. And he knew Jonathan had gone to find out the information which she wanted so badly, to please her. To shut her up. He had said that, ages ago. It's what he had said to him: 'Catch the bastards yourself and prove yourself a hero.' But he'd meant a live hero, not a dead one. Better to be a live coward than a dead hero. Wasn't it?

He shook his head and could feel the tears coming up again, and Mr McNair said, 'Forget it, Elizabeth. He'll tell you when he comes round. It'll be all right in the morning.'

In the morning the news on the telephone was still 'critical' but in the evening the police sent a car for Peter to take him to the hospital.

'He's saying something, but we can't make it out, and we thought—as you seem to know more about it than anyone else—you might be a better person to talk to him.'

'Well—' Peter would rather have not, being a desperate coward when faced with emotional situations; like Jonathan himself, he would rather withdraw and watch the others going through the motions, reserving judgement. They had far more in common than he had thought at first. He realized he was going to miss him desperately when he went, whichever way he was fated to go . . . he couldn't think about it really; it was impossible, in front of the policeman, and he went the rest of the way in grim, teeth-clenched silence.

Like most things deeply dreaded, it wasn't so bad after all. Apart from the fact that he seemed to be attached to a lot of machinery and was lying on his face and not very easy to get at, Jonathan didn't appear to Peter to be much different from usual. A nurse fetched him a chair and he sat down and arranged himself at face level and said, 'Hi. What you bin doin' then?'

Jonathan's eyes, rather hazy, took a long time to focus, like a new-born baby's. When they had at last taken in who it was, he smiled, which also seemed to take a long time. Peter adjusted himself to the slow motion.

'I gather you saw Jamie?'—a dry remark, considering Jonathan's condition—'And the beggar shot you. Not nice.'

'In the backside,' Jonathan said.

Peter laughed.

'But only because—the police came. Quite friendly . . . till then.'

'Yes, I'm sorry, that was my fault, I suppose. Everyone was worried about you, disappearing, and I guessed where you'd gone and told them. It was a bad mistake.'

'Well—' Jonathan's eyes shut and he lay quite a long time without saying anything. Peter got the impression he was gathering his strength, and waited.

His patience was eventually rewarded. 'I got Corder's address. In the back pocket of my jeans.' Jonathan's voice was a whisper, but there was no mistaking the satisfaction.

Peter sat back, grinning. Jonathan's eyes were shut again, but Peter knew, and Jonathan had known, that the interview was concluded. There was nothing to add, the triumph in a nutshell, and Jonathan had lapsed into unconsciousness again. Short and to the point, characteristically Meredith. Peter said to the nurse, 'He will be all right? If it's only his backside—he said that—'

'There's a lot more to it than that, he's doing very well,' the nurse said. 'He's very strong, which helps. Did he say whatever it was they wanted to know?'

'Yes.'

'Good. We'll leave him then.'

'Is Mrs Meredith here?'

'I think so.'

'Has she seen him yet?'

'No. She's so upset, we thought it better not. For him, not her. You're the first person to see him.'

Peter, in spite of everything, kept wanting to laugh . . . Jonathan going, cool as a cucumber, to Jamie and getting the address without any trouble at all, doing what all the professional sleuths of Europe had failed to do, over a mere cup of tea . . . ! If only they hadn't interfered, he'd have hitched home and turned up, pleased as punch, his immediate life's ambition nicely accomplished, and another race to look forward to next Saturday . . . Blast it, Peter thought—that it hadn't turned out like that, when it so easily could have . . .

'Peter!'

Mrs Meredith was standing in front of him—he hadn't noticed, deep in thought, where he had been going.

'I've spoken to him—the police asked me,' he added rapidly, not wanting her to think he was barging in. 'He said Jamie gave him Corder's present address. It's in the back pocket of his jeans.'

'Oh!'

Mrs Meredith sat down, as if the news was too much to take in. She lay back in the waiting-room chair and shut her eyes.

'Peter—'

'Yes?'

'His jeans, he said his jeans?'

'Yes.'

'The back pocket?'

'Yes.'

'Where he was shot. If you'd seen his jeans—all his clothes—when they gave them to me, in a plastic bag, all covered with blood—'

'What did you do with them?'

'I told the nurse to put them in the incinerator.'

Peter felt his mouth drop open. 'No!'

'Anyone would have—if you'd seen them—'

'Perhaps she didn't. We'll ask her.'

They asked her.

'I'll find out. But I daresay that's what happened, if you didn't want them.'

It was what had happened. Mrs Meredith wept. Peter, past being embarrassed any more after his initiation to—his positive wallowing in—what he would once have thought of as impossible situations, sat waiting for a lift home and wondering whether he could possibly explain to the woman why it really didn't matter.

After the first shock, he could see that it was quite funny. The irony of it would be appreciated by Jonathan, he felt sure, but perhaps it would take a long time for it to be accepted by her. Whatever happened afterwards, when it was out of his hands, Jonathan had got what he wanted out of Jamie. Peter suspected that there was more to it than a bit of paper with an address on, but he would never know that for sure. Only guess. Jonathan had done what he wanted; there had been no mistaking the note of achievement, even in a whisper. Peter knew that nothing would change that.

Several days later Peter saw Jonathan again, in much happier circumstances. Jonathan was still face down in bed, but the hardware was down to a mere tube or two and he looked to Peter perfectly back to normal.

'Just a fraud, in here,' Peter said to him. 'Keeping beds from deserving cases. A sore backside—I've got that every day.'

'I might have known better than expect sympathy from you, McNair. Where's the grapes then? Chocolates?'

Peter groped in his anorak pocket and found four peppermints in a scrumpled packet, which he used for Garnet, who was addicted to them.

'One of these? I can't afford goodies—you know my daddy doesn't pay me. Doesn't even let me keep my winnings.'

167

'No? That's tough. Forty quid at Sheppey Hill. Ma's given me mine.'

'Well, she loves you, seeing as you nearly went down the drain. Brought her to her senses.'

Jonathan grinned. 'Yeah, it's nice to be appreciated. Even after burning the vital evidence—she was quite human about it, actually.'

'What did you think, when you heard she'd burned it?'

'I laughed myself stupid.'

'The doctor said afterwards it wouldn't have been decipherable anyway because one of the bullets must have gone right through it. Can't you remember any of it, or didn't you read it first?'

'I remember Australia, and it ends in "gong" or something similar, so it's not entirely in vain. I'm glad Jamie got away, that's all. I'm not bothered about anything else. At least—sorry I can't ride Florestan and beat you properly.'

'I've got to ride them both, starting tomorrow.'

'Yes, I'm sorry about that. Come and tell me, afterwards.'

'That Melissa Jones—' Peter smiled, remembering— 'She told me she fancies you. Dreamy, she said— something about your lovely black curls. "Who is he?" What do you think of that?'

Jonathan's eyes opened very wide. 'You're kidding?'

'No. She said that.'

Jonathan said nothing, but coloured up against the white sheets, smiling.

'There, that's worth more than a bunch of grapes,' Peter said.

'I reckon—yes.'

The news seemed to have struck him dumb, for he lay gazing into space with no more to say. Peter picked a few petals off his chrysanthemums, looked at his watch, and said, 'When are they kicking you out then? I can't waste my time doing a lot of this.'

'Oh, quite soon, I think. They've sorted it all out. It's just a matter of waiting a bit, I think, while it heals.'

'Then what?'

'Well, back to school, I suppose. Seems a bit odd, after all this. Pity to miss the racing though. I'm really sorry about that. Especially if—what you say—'

'Shall I take her a message?'

'What—well, what can I say? It doesn't work like that, does it? I'm not likely to see her again—unless I can get to watch in a car, in a week or two.'

'No. I'll tell her what happened. Work up a bit of sympathy—how brave you were and all that. It was all in the newspapers again, you know, so I expect she saw it. You're a glutton for publicity.'

'Was it? How ghastly! At least they spared me Humphrey this time.'

'Wonder he didn't call and ask for a re-run. Just show us how you were shot in the bottom. Dolly's got the ketchup. What a laugh!'

He looked at his watch again and said, 'I've got to go. Two flaming racehorses to prepare for tomorrow. I do miss you, you know.'

'The work I did, you bet.'

'I'll come tomorrow night and tell you how I got on. If I live to tell the tale.'

'Okay.'

Peter disappeared through the door, and almost immediately came back again. He was grinning like a maniac.

'You've got another visitor waiting—advance warning.' He pulled a comb out of his pocket and offered it. 'Want to arrange your lovely black curls? It's not your mother, that's all I'm saying.'

169

'It's not—?'

Jonathan lifted his head up, looking terrified.

'It is, you know.'

'Oh, Jeez! Peter—hey, don't leave me—'

'In good hands,' Peter said soothingly. 'Only one at a time, it's in the rules.'

Jonathan groaned, lay down again and shut his eyes as if in pain. Then he started to smile.

'You're not joking?' He looked at Peter.

'No. Honest.'

'Okay. Get out then.'

'On my way.'

Peter went to the door and opened it for the lady. 'He's all yours, Miss Jones,' he said.

'Oh, hullo, it's you. Garnet,' she said.

'Yes. Florestan's in there.'

'It's all right—my coming?'

'Yes. Very.'

She smiled and went slightly pink, and went in. She was stunning, Peter thought, and was even a bit jealous. But Jonathan deserved a break where womenfolk were concerned. Peter went down the stairs and met Mrs Meredith at the bottom on her way up. He almost put his arms out to make a barrier, to stop her, but it seemed rather extreme, so he stood in her way and said, grovelling desperately in his pocket for some money, 'Oh, hullo, Mrs Meredith, can I buy you a cup of tea?'

Mrs Meredith looked at him as if he had gone mad.

'I've come to see Jonathan.'

'Yes, but it's so handy, and I was just going to have one.' Peter gestured towards the alcove near the bottom of the stairs where the WVS ladies were doing a good trade with visitors. 'I've been up there and they're doing something to him—they said to wait a bit—'

This brilliant bit of improvisation seemed to convince

170

her, as she turned towards the tea counter and said, 'All right, dear, I'll buy you a cup in that case. I know you're always short of money. There's nothing wrong up there, is there?' she added.

'Oh, no. Just routine servicing. He's fine.'

'Thank goodness. Go and get a couple of seats and I'll get the tea. Cake?'

'Yes please.'

She joined him in a minute with the refreshments, putting a large gooey piece of chocolate cake down in front of Peter, which cheered him up considerably.

'I can't tell you how relieved I am he's out of danger now. It's been such a terrible experience . . .' She stirred her cup of tea slowly, and then said quietly, 'It really has put the whole thing in perspective for me. It doesn't matter any more, not like it did, losing the money. Not as long as Jonathan . . . well, thinking back on it, and I thought a lot while I was waiting around in this place, I think perhaps I was a little hard on him, my attitude, you know. He doesn't show what he's thinking, you see, and one doesn't know what's going on in his head, so one is apt to push him, trying to make him give something away. And the more one pushes, the more he closes up. It's very difficult. Do you know what I mean?'

'Yes.'

'Did he ever say to you . . . did he ever suggest that I was, perhaps, hard on him?'

Peter, his mouth very full of chocolate cake, did not know what to say. He thought of what she had just said, about Jonathan closing up, and thought that Jonathan had the right idea, and said, having swallowed the cake, 'Oh, no. Never.'

'I'm glad. I wouldn't like it thought that I—I drove him. He has his own way to make, after all. I can't do it for him.'

No, Peter thought, and just at this moment he's making his own way pretty well.

'Going to Jamie like that—he must have known it was a very dangerous thing to do. Why didn't he tell the police and leave it to them? I've thought, you see, that perhaps he went for reasons of his own that he hasn't told anyone, even now. And even though he's had such a bad time he's curiously—how shall I put it?—philosophical, perhaps— have you noticed? He seems happier, somehow, as if there was something he was worrying about and now there isn't. Do you have any theories about it? It might be my imagination, I'm not sure.'

'Oh, yes,' said Peter. 'I should think it is. No, I've no theories at all.'

'Do you want another piece of chocolate cake?'

'Yes please.'

'How long are they going to be up there? Did they say?'

'Oh, quite a long time they said. About an hour.'

'Really? How very odd. I suppose I could go and do a bit of shopping while I'm waiting. I didn't really mean to say all this to you. Don't say anything to Jonathan later, will you? I wouldn't like him to think . . . I'll tell you what, if I've got to hang around—how about us going to the Coffee-Pot and I'll buy you one of their peach melbas, to celebrate . . . everything. Would you like that? You appear to be starving.'

'Yes, I would.'

'We'll do that then.' She gathered up her gloves and bag and stood up. She looked at her watch. 'An hour you say?'

'Yes, I think that would do.'

'Very well.'

She marched out, an imposing figure in her winter tweeds, very outdoor and healthy and dominating, and

Peter got up wearily to follow. He thought of Melissa Jones sitting on Jonathan's bed upstairs with a great wrench of envy, remembered the peach melba, grinned, and opened the door for Mrs Meredith. All in all he had arranged the afternoon very well. Jonathan should be grateful.

Other books by K. M. Peyton

A Pattern of Roses
ISBN 0 19 275061 5

The initials on the drawing said T.R.I.—the same as
Tim's. But the drawing was done in 1910 and the initials
belonged to another boy. At the local churchyard Tim
sees his gravestone and tries to unravel the mystery of
Tom's early death. But the deeper Tim delves into the
past, the more Tom Inskip seems to come to life. Is he
sending a message—or is it a warning . . .

A Midsummer Night's Death

ISBN 0 19 271774 X

Jonathan Meredith is stunned by the news that his
English teacher has drowned in the river close to the
school. The coroner's verdict is suicide, but Jonathan
begins to wonder if there is a more sinister reason for the
teacher's death.

As Jonathan gets closer to the truth he starts to
believe his life may also be in danger. And on a rock-
climbing holiday to Wales, his climb up the cliff face
becomes a matter of life and death.

Flambards
ISBN 0 19 275024 0

Twelve-year-old Christina is sent to live in a decaying old mansion with her fierce uncle and his two sons. She soon discovers a passion for horses and riding, but she has to become part of a strange family. This brooding household is divided by emotional undercurrents and cruelty . . .

The Edge of the Cloud

Winner of the Carnegie Medal
ISBN 0 19 275023 2

Christina and Will have run away together, leaving the tense atmosphere of Flambards behind. Will is determined to fly one of the new aeroplanes that are all the rage now, in the early years of the twentieth century, while Christina finds that people frown on a young girl working for a living. Worst of all, Christina realizes that with Will, she will always come second to his passion for machines.

Flambards in Summer
ISBN 0 19 275054 2

Widowed during the First World War, Christina decides
to return to Flambards, the forbidding home of her
childhood. She finds the house is buried in ivy, the
paddocks are a jungle, and the once busy stables are
deserted and desolate. So Christina sets herself the task of
turning it into a successful farm. Together Christina and
Dick, the young groom who first taught her to ride, set
about restoring Flambards to its former glory. But history
returns to haunt them . . .

Flambards Divided
ISBN 0 19 275055 0

The old ivy-covered house of Flambards has seen many
changes since Christina first arrived as a girl of twelve.
With the First World War coming to an end, Christina
feels the time has come to leave the past behind and look
to the future with Dick, the former groom in the stables.
But the local gentry refuse to accept Dick into their society
and when Major Mark Russell returns from the war in
France, Christina finds her feelings divided between these
two very different men in her life.